THE MYSTERY OF THE POINTING DOG

BRENNA BRIGGS

2014

BROCKAGH BOOKS
MINERAL POINT, WISCONSIN, U.S.A.

INTRODUCTION

Irish dancer Liffey Rivers has recently moved to Mineral Point, Wisconsin, where long ago, on November 1, 1842, a public hanging took place. Thousands of people came to watch the gruesome event unfold. The facts in this book concerning the public hanging have been carefully researched. *The Mystery of the Pointing Dog* is historical fiction, interwoven with Liffey Rivers' most challenging and baffling mystery to date.

CHAPTER ONE
Mineral Point
Wiskonsin Territory
November 1, 1842

Jane Scott's head was pounding and she was having difficulty breathing as her older brother, Patrick, dragged her through the Widow Hood's fields of rotting corn. It was hard to keep her footing and not twist an ankle on the decomposing corncobs littering the ground.

A murder of crows, pecking away at the worms tunneling through the Widow's blighted corn, was disturbed by the pounding feet and flew up shrieking, circling widely before settling on the branches of a leafless oak tree.

"Mam told me once that crows are harbingers of death, Patrick," Jane wheezed.

Her brother snickered.

"Them crows are here to eat up the caterpillars in the Widow's bad corn, little Sister, not to warn you and me about a murderer on his way to the gallows."

"Well, Brother," Jane persisted, "we are, after all, on our way to watch that man's death, and just maybe these crows..."

"Whatever you say, little nipper. Them crows are here in the Widow Hood's fields just to warn you and me about the public hanging we already knew about anyways."

Jane squeezed her eyelids into tiny slits, trying to stem the tide of salty sweat streaming down from her forehead before it reached her celery-green eyes.

When they reached the gallows, she would close her eyes completely, because ten-year-old girls such as herself, had no business whatsoever going to watch a public execution like it was a civilized extravaganza.

Just wait 'til I tell Mam that big brother nursemaid made me miss school and pulled me through the Widow Hood's foul cornfields. Calling me a crybaby just because I don't want to go and see a man get hanged...

Jane did not exactly wish to seek revenge against her brother, but after she had sobbed and pleaded with him to let her walk to school alone if he was so set on skipping, she thought he deserved to be held accountable for hijacking her.

She knew from the very beginning that her place

2

at the J. E. Heaton School was coveted by others.

When it had opened its doors two years ago, her mam had sidled up to the front of the registration queue and had managed to enroll Patrick and herself in the first public school in Mineral Point.

Now her brother might have ruined everything. Mr. Heaton did not tolerate truants. As a last resort, she had tried to bite down hard on Patrick's wrist so she could do a scoot into the woods behind the barn and hide out in her secret place.

But she had missed her brother's arm and bitten down on her own delicate hand instead.

This clumsy, self-inflicted injury, fueled her rage. Today she was not only truant from school, now she was also an injured truant. *We'll just see who the crybaby is when Mam finds out.*

Jane thought that she understood the saying 'an eye for an eye and a tooth for a tooth' because her parish priest, Father Samuel Mazzuchelli, had talked about it in a sermon one Sunday when he was saying a Station Mass over at Foster's shanty.

He said those words came right from the Old Testament. But then, later on, Jesus preached that we must forgive our enemies—if someone slapped you on the right cheek, you should turn your head and let him slap you on the left one too.

WHY would anybody in their right head ever do that?

It was all very confusing.

How could her best friend, Mary Southwick, just

go and forgive the man who had shot and killed her favorite uncle? The one who had always given her the nicest presents, and saffron, the most expensive spice in the whole world, for her family's Christmas buns.

And just let her ignorant brother even try to slap her in the face or anywhere else for that matter.

She would fight right back.

First, I would kick him hard in both kneecaps and when he was down on the ground I would…

It seemed logical to Jane, though, that hanging Mr. Caffee today was neither going to bring Mary's uncle back to life again, nor fix her broken heart.

By the time they finally reached the edge of Mineral Point, Jane Scott could barely walk and her copper curls had gone limp.

"Looks like the badgers up here have already set out, Jane. Let's get a move on," Patrick mumbled, oblivious to his sister's precarious physical condition.

Jane looked at the gaping holes in the surrounding hills, trying to imagine what life was like for many of the local miners who burrowed into the hillsides each winter, like badgers, to survive the cold.

She was delighted to see that this afternoon, all of the wood-fired lead smelter ovens in town appeared to have been shut down.

That's the one and only good thing about this hanging day, she thought. *I'm not gagging on smoke.*

Brother and sister passed by the site where the first Catholic house of worship in Mineral Point was being erected. It was going to be called 'Saint Paul's,' just like her da's first name, but "you leave out the 'Saint' part," Mam had laughed.

Jane made the sign of the cross with her free hand to show respect, like Mam said you should do when you passed by a Catholic church. She hoped that Patrick had not noticed because he might make fun of her since the church was not actually there yet.

If he does laugh at me, I might just give him that chance to turn his other cheek....

When they arrived at the top of High Street's hill and looked down into Mineral Point, it looked like every single person in Iowa County, except for their parents, had come out today to watch the gruesome event unfold.

A disturbing thought occurred to Jane. What if their parents were here in this mob too and had just *said* they were going shopping in Dodgeville today because they did not want their children to know where they were really going?

Jane cringed. *No, Mam would never want to see a man get hanged. But Da?*

She banished this disturbing thought and studied the horizon. Even if it had been possible to see the flat area around the corner at the bottom of the hill where the scaffold had been built the night before, today there was a low-lying haze of lingering smoke obstructing the view.

I wish I could have seen this town before they started cutting the trees down to burn in their smelly lead ovens.

Unless there was a strong wind blowing the smoke away, visibility from any distance in Mineral Point in 1842 was almost impossible on most days.

It would serve my brother right if he goes through all this trouble of half killing me and does not get to watch that man hang after all, Jane thought.

As if on cue, a westerly wind came up, sending the leftover puffs of smoke off to the east, revealing the unfolding spectacle below.

Jane found it hard to believe that there were so many morbidly curious sight-seers spilling into town from every direction. They came in wagons and on horseback and foot. There were mothers with babes in arms and young children in tow. She shook her head disapprovingly. *Grown women ought to know better.*

"Look Patrick, I can see men up on the roof of the Land Office and the hills up ahead look like they have worms crawling all over them, like the Widow's bad corn!" Jane exclaimed, shaking her head again, wondering why anyone would be voluntarily coming here for this hanging—and with picnic baskets yet!

"Looks like John Phillips' brewery and General Smith's tavern most likely have full roofs too," Jane sighed.

"And, it looks like the Cousin Jacks are coming to watch," Patrick added, steering his sister past several clusters of Cornish miners in their broad brimmed hats who were making their way over from Shake Rag Street towards the gallows.

Jane glanced over her shoulder and saw that a few

6

of the spinsters from church were walking directly behind them through the swelling crowd.

The pious Sunday morning fusspots were giggling and whispering, acting like giddy school girls passing secrets to each other.

Why do those holy biddies want to go and watch a man get hanged? They came here today of their own free will. Not one of them is being dragged here like me.

One late night a few weeks ago, when her parents thought she was asleep up in the loft above the kitchen, Jane had listened to her mam and da talking about the murder of Mr. Samuel Southwick, and how he and his murderer, Mr. William Caffee, had been guests at Captain Fortunatus Berry's house-warming ball over at Gratiot's Grove.

From what Jane could make out, apparently Mr. Caffee had become very angry because he thought that his name had not been called out to dance. He insisted that there would be no more dancing until he heard "**C-A-F-F-E-E**" called out loud and clear. He did not believe it when he was told that his name had already been called but he had not come forward.

"So Mr. Caffee grabbed the set dance list and ran outside with it. I figure he must have been thinking that if he could not dance, then nobody could," Da said.

Her mam said that the church gossips had heard that Mr. Caffee, who was only thirty years old, was already known to be a disorderly drunk over at White

Oak Springs and that he often used vile, threatening language like, "I'll cut your heart out," if someone got under his skin.

Da said he had heard that most of the witnesses who had testified in Judge Dunn's courtroom at the Caffee murder trial had said that Mr. Southwick and several other men had grabbed pieces of stove wood and run outside after Mr. Caffee to get the dance set list back.

"Caffee must have thought that Samuel Southwick was ready to strike and shot him first," Mam said.

Da agreed with Mam. He said that he thought that Moses Strong, Mr. Caffee's lawyer, had tried his best to get his drunken, irresponsible client a jury verdict of 'Justifiable Homicide,' but the jury did not see it that way.

After he fired his pistol, Da said that Mr. Caffee had run away to Saint Louis on horseback, until the bounty hunters found him there and he was brought back to Mineral Point to stand trial.

Jane could tell from her mam's voice that she was heartsick about all the sad things that had happened. She blamed Mr. Southwick's unfortunate demise on demon liquor and how it sometimes made ordinarily God-fearing people do terrible, terrible things.

Mam thought that there should be a Temperance Society organized right here in Iowa County, like the one in Milwaukee.

"And now, along with all that demon whiskey and John Phillips brewing all that sinful beer up on that hill, everywhere you turned, there was that hard apple cider being made by all those short Cousin Jennys."

Jane crawled out of bed and looked down at her parents through a crack in the floor. She had never noticed that the Cornish women in town were short.

She could see Mam plaiting her long red hair into a thick braid while she went rattling on.

"And why, pardon my asking you, Mr. Scott, do those Cousin Jennys shake rags out their windows every blessed day of the year to signal to their men folk up in the hills that supper is ready? Have they not heard of a dinner bell?"

"And can you for one single minute even believe that those Jennys think *toad dung* makes their apple cider taste better?" Mam wrinkled her nose.

Jane shuddered.

What did her mam mean? Toad dung?

Da pointed out that up until the Cornish miners had come here and built their stone cottages, Mineral Point mostly had poorly built log cabins and thrown-together shacks.

He said the men from Cornwall were deep diggers who had mined tin and copper far under the ground.

"Many Cousin Jacks are skilled stonemasons as well as miners, and they have brought some much needed civilized living to this area," Da said, stifling a yawn.

Jane was beginning to get sleepy while her mother continued talking about how all those short Cousin Jennys put common field toads into their barrels of

9

fermenting apples so that their hard cider would taste better.

"I will tell you one thing for certain, Paul Scott. Those Cousin Jacks and their Jennys will *never, ever,* replace our Saint Patrick with their Cornish Saint Piran!"

Da mumbled some response to Mam's toad talk as he set off for bed.

Jane pulled herself back up into her own bed and tucked herself in under the soft quilt Mam had made for her birthday last year.

CHAPTER TWO
Mineral Point
Wisconsin Today

L iffey Rivers squeezed her eyelids into tiny slits, attempting to shield her eyes from the sharp blasts of a pitiless wind, as she made her way down High Street to the Red Rooster Café.

The local weather station had reported that today was the coldest November first in Mineral Point's history, but that by the end of the day, temperatures would rise again, bringing heavy, wet snow, which would then turn into freezing rain.

A grand finale with thunder, lightning and black ice was expected, followed by heavy fog, after which a warm front would move in.

An animated meteorologist had concluded: "It's going to be a Snowmageddon."

Liffey had almost reached the gray metal pointer dog jutting out above the entrance to the Gray Dog Deli, when the wind started moaning pitifully, like her dog Max did if he caught her trying to sneak out of the house without him.

Max the Magnificent was only a small terrier but he could howl louder than a large bloodhound and act 'pathetic' better than any movie star dog.

A powerful surge of wind roared up High Street, adding another foot of heavy snow to the immense pile already blocking Liffey's path.

Liffey considered using her Irish dance training and doing a leapover to launch herself over this new snow hill, but it kept shape-shifting and she was in no mood to slip and fall down because she had an Irish dance competition next weekend. She was not going to risk a self-inflicted injury.

When the gray dog, hardly visible through the blowing snow, loomed directly above her, she cupped her hands and called up: "What do you say, Mr. Gray Dog? Is this the worst November first in Mineral Point's history? I've heard that you've been here since 1871, so you must have an educated opinion by now."

Maybe this gray zinc dog would have preferred standing down on the sidewalk where it had greeted people in front of the Gundry & Gray Department Store long ago? It looked cold and lonely standing up there on its iron platform, far away from the friendly pats of sidewalk passersby.

Before Liffey had figured out the best way to get around the mound of snow, waves of sunlight rolled through the opaque snow clouds and a shadow, cast by the gray dog, appeared on the snow drift that was blocking her way.

Though the statue of the gray dog was pointing uphill, its shadow appeared to be traveling downhill.

This is totally weird. It's got to be some kind of mirage, like when you're lost in the middle of a desert, dying of thirst, and you start seeing palm trees and pools of water that are not really there, Liffey thought uneasily.

She consciously ignored the prickling sensations that had started creeping up her spine when the dog's shadow had started moving.

When she heard a plow truck at the very bottom of High Street churning its way slowly uphill, she hurriedly crossed over to the other side of the street, to avoid more snow from being dumped in her path.

Liffey happily noted that the shadow of the dog had apparently not crossed over with her to this side of High Street and that the wind had finally stopped howling.

She must be sane after all.

Something seemed different on this other side of the street. It was very quiet over here—like standing in the middle of a pine forest with softly falling snow, expecting something to happen.

A whispering wind was nudging her, suggesting

that she practice her hop-one-two-threes, but she was already busy catching fat snowflakes on her tongue.

Although she was very much enjoying her new hushed surroundings and the respite this side of the street provided from the storm, she was confused. When she looked across the street at the Gray Dog Deli, she saw large funnel clouds of snow. The storm was raging over there and the plow she had avoided by quickly crossing the street, had deposited, as she knew it would, at least another foot of snow on the sidewalk underneath the pointer dog.

She wondered.

Had she tried to do an Irish dance leapover after all over that pile of snow?

Had she then slipped and hit her head? She felt for a goose egg. There wasn't one.

Was she down on the ground unconscious now? Slowly freezing to death underneath an avalanche of snow and only imagining everything was peaceful and lovely over here on this 'other' side of the street?

That had to be it! She had gone down trying to do the leapover. She must have a serious head injury.

She needed to wake up before she froze to death under the snowdrift across the street.

Liffey decided, however, that she was going to stay over here on this mellow side of the street for as long as she could.

She was curious as to why she could not see the Red Rooster sign. She should be able to see it clearly because there was no blizzard on this side of High

Street.

Now that she thought about it, there were way fewer buildings on this side of the street too, and they seemed much smaller and were mostly made out of wood. Where had all the stone buildings gone?

It was very soothing over here, with or without all the buildings, and Liffey wondered when, or if, she would wake up.

It really didn't matter much.

All at once, the snow disappeared on both sides of the street and it was no longer cold. The sky was indigo blue, dotted with fleecy clouds and the sun shone brightly. Beginning to overheat, she slipped out of her heavy winter parka and analyzed her altered surroundings.

There were large groups of people now, laughing and shouting to each other as they moved hurriedly down High Street which was now a dirt road. Some rode in horse-drawn wagons, but they were not the black box buggies that the Amish around here used. Where had all these people come from?

There must have been several thousand of them but not one of them glanced over at her standing on the sidewalk—where was the sidewalk?

When she looked down, she could see that she was now standing on thick planks of wood.

Overwhelmed with curiosity, she waved, trying to get the attention of a tall, handsome boy who was passing by only a few feet away. He was pulling a pretty, freckle-faced little girl along behind him. She was wearing a green dress that looked like it belonged on a Raggedy Ann doll. Poor little thing. She looked overheated and exhausted. Liffey felt invisible as no one seemed to notice her.

It slowly dawned on Liffey that this crowd was wearing very odd clothing—the women wore down-to-the-ankle, dark dresses. The men were dressed in either ill-fitting, three-piece suits or long-sleeved gray shirts tucked into gray trousers. The children were all dressed like the old fashioned porcelain dolls she had seen before in museums.

Could it still be Halloween? Mineral Point had a Halloween costume parade each year but that was yesterday. She remembered clapping for her school's band as they marched by playing "On Wisconsin." She had been wearing her Zorro mask and her mother's Spanish Gaucho hat. That had all happened yesterday.

But then again, maybe not.

She was not going to worry about a technicality.

It was really very nice being over here, wherever she was.

Before Liffey could figure out who these people were and get a grip, she began to feel like she was riding a horse on a slowly moving merry-go-round at an amusement park, watching things go by.

Suddenly, the huge crowd of people vanished like a puff of smoke, and the dreamy quality of life on this side of the street was totally gone—driven off by the return of the oppressive snow storm now raging on both sides of High Street. Shivering, she pulled her parka on again.

She still had no memory of actually falling down and hitting her head, even though she knew that must have happened. But if she *had* fallen down, then how had she managed to get over here on this Red Rooster side of the street while she was unconscious over on the Gray Dog side?

Logically, she should have awakened on the Gray Dog side of the street, not the Red Rooster side.

Before she could think of a rational explanation, the wind died down enough so she could see the Red Rooster Café's sign with its flat, red metal bird jutting up like a lighthouse a few yards away.

When Liffey's father had announced out of the blue that he had retired, sold his law firm along with their lake house and they were relocating to Mineral Point, she was taken by surprise. But any misgivings she had were resolved quickly when she realized that at last she would be escaping from the black hole where she had lived and suffered since the beginning of time.

So far, living in Mineral Point had been great.

Her architect mother described their new town as a patchwork quilt of period buildings.

Lovely limestone cottages, built by people from Cornwall in the 1800's, lined the streets of the Point and the city was surrounded by rolling green hills that reminded Liffey of Ireland.

Parent-enforced family 'outings' were pleasant—

even fun here. Amish buggies often appeared around bends in the roads and her little brother, Neil, never stopped looking out of the back window with his binoculars, hoping to spot one of the black bears that occasionally wandered into Iowa County.

Mineral Point was a smoothie of potters, poets, knitters, painters, writers, sculptors, weavers, quilters, actors and photographers, all blended together.

At Shake Rag Alley, where miners' wives in the 1800's shook rags from their cottage windows to signal to the men in the hills across the street that supper was waiting, there were now workshops held all year round. Concerts and plays were performed during the summer on the large outdoor stage built into a limestone cliff.

But by far the best thing about living in Mineral Point, was that there was no Principal Godzilla at the local high school to make her life miserable.

Liffey's parents had decided that it was time for her to attend a regular school again. They told her that Aunt Jean, who had homeschooled Liffey while her mother was hospitalized in Ireland, needed to get back to her own life again. But Liffey knew that it was really because her Aunt Jean's teaching methods were very unusual. Robert Rivers had used the word "outrageous."

Liffey missed her aunt's strange obsessions with Irish dancing and top fashion models and chasing bad energy from rooms. She had recently told Liffey about a new solo dress she was designing for her

18

adult Irish dancing competitions. Apparently, Aunt Jean had invented a lever that released butterfly wings when she did her airborne Slip Jig steps.

Liffey was very interested in seeing how these wings worked and possibly even designing wings for herself to use if she faced a steps emergency at a feis. Anything that might distract feis judges should be investigated, even though she knew full well that her mother would never tolerate such tactics.

However, since she and her Aunt Jean sometimes went off alone to feiseanna, if her mother could not come, the wings were something she might be able experiment with under the right circumstances.

At first, it was very hard waking up for regular high school classes. Liffey had to force herself to get out of bed each morning and she missed sleeping in until noon when her aunt's 'School of Life' modules began each day.

On the positive side of things, even though the high school in Mineral Point was very small, she had already made several friends, which was a big first for Liffey.

Up until now, the only real friends she had ever made lived far away. Her BFF Sinead McGowan was a whole continent away in County Sligo, Ireland. And John Bergman, a boy she had met on an Alaskan cruise last spring, and the only boy she had ever known that she actually enjoyed talking with, lived in New Hampshire, over a thousand miles away from Mineral Point.

Even though they all kept in touch, it was nice to have some new friends who actually lived in the same place she did for a change.

Liffey knew that her new friend, Susan Scott, who had been pestering her to try something called 'figgy hobbin' and 'pasties' at the Red Rooster Café, was totally on to her not wanting to taste either dish. She had texted Liffey last night to meet up with her for lunch. Liffey supposed that today was as good as any other day to have her showdown with the figgy food. Susan had also said that there was a confusing puzzle she needed help with solving and Liffey could not resist having a go at it.

In spite of this blizzard, random hallucinations, possible serious head injury and figgy whatever, the prospect of a brain-twister propelled Liffey onward, towards the Red Rooster.

Long slivers of sharp sunlight scratched through dark clouds and the faint shadow of the red metal rooster on the sign above her appeared on curbside snow. This time, Liffey hardly reacted. It was only a shadow. Before she had time to think '*déjà vu*,' the rooster's shadow began to twirl round and round like a spinning top until it began to look more like the shadow of a wagging tail of a dog.

Liffey tried to convince herself that she was not actually seeing what happened next—the wagging tail trailing behind the shadow of a tall man sauntering downhill, just a few feet past the Red Rooster Café.

20

Great. Now I'm seeing a human hallucination. I so hit my head...

Even worse than her hallucinations, this was the second time today that the small hairs on her arms were standing up on alert.

Up until this moment, Liffey had been thankful for the uneventful life she had been happily leading since moving to the Point.

For the first time ever, a feeling of contentment and normalcy had entered her turbulent life. She had a father and a mother and a little brother and Max the Magnificent and Irish dancing and her crazy Aunt Jean and friends.

There were white and purple lilac bushes planted around her new house and next spring, Liffey and her mother would go outside to inhale their lovely fragrance every morning, just like they had done so many years ago before her mother had gone missing.

Surely nothing bad could be starting up in her life again so soon?

But if not, then why all the prickling sensations? She never had them unless there was danger lurking somewhere close by.

No. That was not it. This time, there had to be another explanation.

Trouble for Liffey Rivers was totally yesterday. It was ancient history.

Liffey braced herself against what now seemed like a hurricane force wind and tried to pull the Red Rooster's door open.

21

She already felt the pasty meat pie and whatever figgy hobbin might be, rising up from the pit of her queasy stomach.

CHAPTER THREE
Hanging Day

Tuesday, the first of November, 1842, was an unseasonably warm mid-60's day in Mineral Point, Wiskonsin Territory.

Since it was already late autumn, most of the spectators who were crammed together around the gallows and up on the surrounding hill slopes, had expected it to be chilly and were overdressed.

Jane desperately wished now that her dim-witted brother had thought to bring along a canteen filled with water because her mouth was drier than dust.

Even though the heat had slowed Patrick down, he had still managed to pull his little sister, in her first store-bought green calico dress, all the way to the front of the loud, expectant crowd at the bottom of

High Street.

Within minutes of Patrick's claiming one of the best eyewitness spots to be had in the unruly mob, a tsunami hush washed over the expectant audience when the clip-clopping of iron-clad horses' hooves sounded off in the distance.

It was happening.

Jane took a deep breath and shut her eyes.

She kept them closed tightly as Patrick described Major Gray's local cavalry riding by on their shiny black horses, dressed in fancy parade attire, sabers dangling at their sides.

It was a struggle not to open her eyes for a brief moment and take it all in because Jane loved horses. But her brother had warned her that the murderer and his coffin would be arriving on a horse-pulled wagon on his trip from the jail to the gallows and she was not about to take in such an awful sight.

Patrick said that next, coming up from behind the cavalry, was Colonel Sublett's troop of Infantry men. Behind the Infantry troop, a marching band stepped along, instruments pressed to lips, fingers on valves and slides, ready to play.

She held her breath and her pulse quickened when she heard the sound of squeaking wheels blending together with the snorting of horses pulling what had to be a wagon. It was close.

Jane jumped when the band that had just passed by her started playing a loud, somber dead march. Before she knew it, the horse-drawn wagon sounded like it was directly in front of her and she could hear pounding noises, like someone on the wagon was trying to keep time with the gloomy music.

Before she could stop them, Jane's eyes popped open and she saw a wild-eyed man, wearing a long white robe and white hooded hat, sitting on top of a pinewood casket.

He was drumming on both sides of his coffin with two empty bottles. Sheriff George Messersmith, along with two of his deputies, sat on opposite sides of the doomed man, controlling his movements with a knotted rope they had wrapped around his scrawny neck.

Jane gulped and stepped back. She reached for Patrick's arm but he had fainted and slumped down to the ground.

The church busybodies, who had elbowed their way up to the front of the crowd with them, revived Patrick with water from the canteen that prissy Miss Know-It-All-Adams had packed in their large picnic basket.

Serves my bullying brother right, Jane thought smugly, lifting her chin up while she struggled to control her own emotions.

"Patrick, drink up some of this water and you'll be your old self again," said Miss Bridget O'Hare, a dark haired, pleasant young woman who always wore a lovely smile on her face. It was hard to believe she was still wearing that smile after what had just passed by. Even harder to figure why she was so friendly with those other sour pusses.

Jane shuddered and shut her eyes again, hugging herself tightly, trying to control the violent trembling that had taken hold of her limbs.

Not far away, she could hear Mr. Caffee quietly cursing and making idle threats. Then he shifted to a loud voice and proclaimed that Mineral Point was hanging an innocent man today because he had only acted in self-defense.

There was a long silence after William Caffee's outburst. Only impatient horses' hooves pawing on the hard dirt road and the scattered sobs of women throughout the crowd, apparently regretting now that they had come to witness this public hanging, could be heard.

Jane was taken aback when she recognized the voice of Mary Southwick's minister, the Reverend Mr. Wilcox, from the Methodist Church. He was reciting Psalm 23 from the Bible about going down into the valley of death. Jane had never liked this particular Psalm. She did not think it was comforting.

One Sunday, not long after Mr. Southwick had been murdered and Father Samuel Mazzuchelli was saying Mass somewhere else in the Wiskonsin Territory, she had participated in the Methodist Church's Sunday worship with Mary Southwick to lend her bereaved friend moral support.

Afterwards, she thought about how grateful she was that she was Catholic and not Methodist because

Mary's Methodist service had lasted over two hours, and Father Mazzuchelli, who only came every few months to pray a Station Mass at somebody's house, was usually finished up with the Mass *and* preaching in about thirty minutes flat.

Mam told her that Father Mazzuchelli always had to rush things because he was the only priest within hundreds of miles and he had to say more masses before dark in other parts of the Territory.

From far off, a familiar hymn began to swell up and fluttered over the massive crowd like a choir of low-flying angels. It was Elder William Roberts and his church group singing *Jerusalem, My Happy Home*.

Jane could feel her brain starting to spin out of control into a kind of tornado tizzy waiting for this hanging event to be over with.

Crazy, disjointed thoughts were racing through her head like one of the Bach fugues Mr. Heaton had played during his organ recital at the Welsh church three Sundays ago.

She did not think Catholics sang Elder Billy's *Happy Jerusalem* hymn but acknowledged to herself that perhaps that was because Father Mazzuchelli wanted only songs with Latin words and he most likely never had had the time to translate *Jerusalem, My Happy Home* into the Latin language because he was always busy traveling throughout the Territory.

She strongly suspected that the church biddies only liked singing the Latin hymns so much because

27

Latin made them feel all educated.

Mam had told her that the creek near the middle of town was named 'Jerusalem Springs' because of this hymn about the happy Jerusalem that Elder Billy and his group were always singing. She said that he was a miner-preacher and also a good man, if a bit odd.

Mam had also told her that Mr. Caffee was not known to be a regular churchgoer but he was from Kentucky, and people from down there were mostly Bible believers.

Jane's head had almost stopped spinning out of control by the time the Reverend Wilcox was done reading Psalm 23 and had switched over to leading the Our Father. But he called it the Lord's Prayer. Father Mazzuchelli said it in Latin and he called it the *Pater Noster*.

Reverend Wilcox's intense, booming voice made Jane imagine what a ringmaster in a circus Big Top tent might sound like when he introduced circus acts, or perhaps an actor, reciting a long speech called a soliloquy from a play by William Shakespeare, on a stage in Chicago.

A dog began to howl.

At last there was a clicking sound, followed by a loud *WHOOSH* and then a flapping noise like her family's laundry made on windy days when it was hanging outside on the clothesline to dry.

A fly buzzed.

CHAPTER FOUR
The Red Rooster Café

Liffey was competing with the wind, trying to pull the Red Rooster's door open, when the long arm of a man with a large hand, wearing a long, gray-sleeved shirt, turned up out of nowhere and held it ajar for her as she teetered inside.

She turned around to thank the helpful man, but he was gone. When she looked outside, all she could see was a long arm followed by a dog's wagging tail, disappearing into the blizzard.

Liffey tried not to think about what had happened to the rest of their bodies.

This is what the Hobbits must have felt like when they left the Shire. One creepy, terrifying thing after another....

Liffey was hoping to forget about her iffy mental health for the moment and have a look at the odd puzzle Susan had texted her about last night.

"I'm back here, Liffey!" Susan called out from

somewhere inside the Rooster, snapping Liffey back into the moment.

Liffey had always been impressed by her friend Susan's almost picture-perfect appearance. Usually, there was not so much as one strand of her auburn hair out of place and her clothes always looked like they had just come off a mannequin in a department store display. No wrinkles. No wear and tear.

Today, however, her friend looked unkempt and frazzled. A Pebbles Flintstone ponytail rose up from her head like a geyser and her light blue sweater had a large hole in the right armpit and only one button.

Liffey was not going to fill Susan in about her odyssey to the Red Rooster today. It was far too complicated and Liffey instinctively knew that if she attempted to describe what had, or might have really happened, Susan might think that she had suffered a traumatic head injury when she jumped over that pile of snow. If she actually *had* tried that leapover.

Liffey smiled cheerfully and waved, trying her best to look upbeat, like she was actually glad to be inside this restaurant that looked like a shrine to poultry.

Wallpaper checkered with chickens decorated the Rooster's walls as she moved past the long Formica lunch counter slicing through the center of the cafe.

When she drew near, Liffey could see that Susan was studying legal-sized papers which she had spread out all over the table. She hardly glanced up as she beckoned Liffey to sit down.

Liffey tried not to look at the dark red **'There is**

always room for Figgy Hobbin' T-shirt hanging on a nearby wall.

What was with this figgy hobbin thing? It sounded like a dish Frodo Baggins and his friends would order for dinner at The Prancing Pony.

Since Liffey had not actually sat down yet, she considered slipping away, especially since her friend looked so preoccupied and the topic of food had not yet come up.

Susan, however, seemed to have anticipated the possibility of Liffey's chickening out and said, "I've already ordered one pasty for us to split and two figgy hobbins—a whole one for each of us. My treat!"

Trying to say something polite, Liffey managed to stammer: "Whoa! Wow! Thanks! That's really so nice of you!"

Susan smiled absently and returned to the papers on the table in front of her.

Liffey reluctantly sat down. "This is it then?"

"Yep. It's a totally weird poem or riddle or puzzle or whatever, illustrated with strange cartoons," Susan answered.

"Uncle William's attorney called a family meeting yesterday and handed out copies of what she said is a 'codicil.' It's an addition to my uncle's main will."

"Anyway, he's drawn a dog, a rooster, some kind of Oriental letters, a fox riding on a horse chasing a man and a tea or coffee cup with a spoon. His poem says that there's a gold mine out there waiting for one of us Scotts to find."

"Do you mind if I have a look at it?" Liffey asked.

"Be my guest! I can't make any sense out of it and it's making my mother crazy. My dad is still too sick to get very much involved," Susan said.

Liffey pulled up closer to the table to get a better look at the peculiar document.

"His will left a third of his house and possessions to each of his nephews—my dad and his two older brothers. This codicil might just be a waste of time. Maybe he had dementia and we just didn't notice— he often couldn't even remember what figgy hobbin was here at the Rooster," Susan said.

Drawing in a controlled breath, Liffey plastered an understanding, sympathetic expression on her face. *Why was Susan always talking about figgy hobbin? It was not normal.*

She continued listening to her friend, trying not to worry about the figgy hobbin that would be coming out of the kitchen any time now.

She had to stop fixating on figgy hobbin.

If she couldn't eat it, so what?

What was the big deal?

Susan wasn't going to hate her if she didn't like it.

"My parents said I could bring the codicil with me to lunch. So please have a go at it!" Susan offered again.

Liffey picked up page one and began to read:

A Codicil to
THE LAST WILL AND
TESTAMENT
OF
WILLIAM ARTHUR SCOTT

IN THE NAME OF GOD, AMEN.

I, William Arthur Scott, do hereby declare this to be a codicil to My LAST WILL AND TESTAMENT hereby revoking any and all other codicils thereto:

I. When the Gray Dog barks

Page one of four pages.

AND THE RED ROOSTER CROWS,

肉餅每天去還是在這裡吃£

II. THE HUNT WILL COMMENCE AND OFF YOU WILL GO!

Page two of four pages.

III. THE WHYs AND WHEREFORES WILL ALL INTERSECT AT THE GOLD MINE YOU WILL FIND TO INSPECT.

Page three of four pages.

IV. GOOD LUCK
AND MAY THE BEST NEPHEW (OR HIS ISSUE) FIND THE TREASURE!

Signed: <u>*William Arthur Scott*</u>

Witnesses: <u>*Ellen Marie Carter*</u>
<u>*Thomas B. Carter*</u>

P.S. Finders Keepers. Losers Weepers. Tom, Dick or Harry: You already have your one third of all my earthly goods. Winner keeps all!

Page four of four Pages.

CHAPTER FIVE
Riddles

"There are gold mines around here?" Liffey asked in a high-pitched voice she hardly recognized.

"Nooo… I wish!" Susan replied.

"The very first thing they teach you in geography class around this place is that Mineral Point is located in what's called the 'Driftless Area' because glaciers did not drift here and flatten us."

"But," Susan went on, "there used to be lots of gray-gold mines—gray-gold is lead. Then later, lots of zinc and a few copper mines, but as far as I am aware, I don't think that anyone ever found any gold around here that was worth anything."

"So then, what do you think your uncle is trying to say in this codicil to his will?"

"Is he just messing with his nephews' heads with these strange cartoons and the weird poem?"

"Did your dad and his brothers get along with your uncle?"

"Tom, Dick or Harry? Are they for real?"

Liffey caught herself, realizing she had begun to sound like an obnoxious trial lawyer cross-examining a hostile witness on the stand.

"Yikes! I sound just like my dad! I'm so sorry, Susan!"

37

Susan laughed good naturedly. "I'm afraid the names are for real. My grandparents had a great sense of humor, depending on the way that you looked at it. They named their three sons after the tortoises Charles Darwin brought back to England with him when he returned from the Galapagos Islands in 1835."

"On the HMS Beagle, right?" Liffey interjected.

"How in the world did you know that, Liffey?"

"My father read me Darwin's *Voyage of the Beagle* when I was eleven," Liffey explained.

"Well then, did you know that later Harry turned out to be a Harriet?" Susan asked.

"Fill me in," Liffey said, sensing that her friend really wanted to tell the rest of this story even though Liffey herself did know the ending.

"So, Harriet lived to be 175 years old in a zoo in Australia. She died in 2006," Susan said.

"As to the question about everybody getting along, I think my uncles liked Uncle Bill okay and I know my dad got along with him really well. My dad is with the FBI and Uncle William worked for the CIA. I think. He never discussed his work but I am pretty sure he was some kind of spy."

"My dad was my uncle's favorite nephew and I know I was his favorite niece. Harry, my dad, is the baby of his family and there's a big age gap."

"We usually had Uncle Bill for Sunday dinners and my mother would always send him home with the leftovers and bring him frozen casseroles all during the week because he was not eating properly. A few months before he died, he refused to leave his house. It was like he became really paranoid or something. So I would stop by here after school on Tuesdays and Thursdays and carry out two figgy hobbins and take them over to his house. It was a standing order at the Rooster until he died last week."

"Did your great uncle speak Chinese, Susan?" Liffey asked, looking again at the Oriental symbols above the rooster illustration and the one by itself on page four.

"Not that I know of," Susan replied. "How can you be sure that these letters are Chinese and not Japanese or Korean, Liffey?"

Liffey had to think a moment about why she was suddenly such an authority on Asian languages.

"Honestly, Susan, I think it's just because I eat shrimp fried rice at Chinese restaurants all the time and I have studied their menus since I was little—especially the ones in London's Chinatown."

"They don't baby you over there like the Chinese restaurants do here with their English translations. I just got used to their letters, or I guess you should call them characters, or symbols."

"The word at the very end of the codicil means 'rooster' in Chinese. Since I was born in the Year of the Rooster, I always practice writing 'rooster' on Zodiac placemats in Chinese restaurants. Everybody needs a hobby, right?"

Susan agreed, impressed with her friend's Chinese

translator credentials.

"Speaking of characters, my Uncle William was quite a character himself," Susan said, picking up the topic again.

"He may have spoken Chinese fluently and never even thought to mention it to the family. As I already told you, he worked in some kind of government intelligence and always told incredible stories about all of the exotic places he had been to and his 'unclassified' adventures."

"My family was never sure about what had really happened in his life or what he had *imagined* had happened—past and present."

"For example, he told my father once when he was a little boy, that we Scotts are related to William Caffee, the man who was hanged here on November 1, 1842—right down at the bottom of High Street across the street near the stream. I guess I thought of that because today is the anniversary of the hanging."

Before Liffey could ask Susan *why* the man had been executed and how he was related to the Scott family, she chattered on: "I do know Uncle William loved living in Mineral Point though, because, just in case you haven't noticed yet, there are some truly unconventional people walking around here, so he fit right in!"

Liffey smiled.

Susan hemmed and hawed a bit before she added, "I think Uncle William even believed all those weird stories about the vampire sightings here too, because he…"

"The *what* sightings?" Liffey asked incredulously. *Hangings and vampires? What kind of place is this?*

"I know it sounds crazy," Susan said, "but some local, underage students back in 1981, told the police that they had seen a real vampire in the Graceland Cemetery, at night, after the gate had been locked. They admitted to the police that they had gone there to smoke. If it hadn't really happened, then why would they go and report it and get themselves in trouble?"

"So, an officer goes to check it out another night and he sees the thing too! He said he chased it as far as the barbed wire fence line at the very back of the cemetery and then lost sight of it after whatever it was jumped effortlessly over the back fence and disappeared."

"The totally creepy thing is that the officer said he used a high power flashlight and could see that there were no footprints in the snow on the other side of the fence!"

Liffey felt a current of excitement racing through her like when she was on a roller coaster climbing up a huge hill, knowing that at any moment, she would be plunging down the other side going 125 miles per hour.

"Then, 27 years later, everything started up again." Susan was becoming more animated as she went on with the story.

"Tell me! What happened the *next* time?" Liffey's

self-control was evaporating and she almost shrieked.

Susan picked up speed: "A vampire jumped out of some tree branches in front of an apartment building a few times and scared people half to death."

"And another time, it crawled up from underneath a dock over at Ludden Lake where a girl and boy were night fishing. At first, they thought they were hearing an animal clawing around underneath the boards. Then, IT climbed up out of the water on the dock's ladder and they almost collapsed. The girl ran away while her boyfriend shone a flashlight in the vampire's white face. Naturally, he panicked too and threw it at the thing and then ran after his girlfriend."

"Please, promise me that you are not making all this up, right?" Liffey implored, trying not to squeal with delight.

"Nope. They're all true stories. You can find them online. Look them up. I mean it might not *all* be true but it supposedly really happened. So…the vampire chases after the guy but the guy manages to drive off with his girlfriend, unharmed. They went straight to the police station and reported it but nothing ever turned up. The vampire obviously did not want to hurt anyone because it never actually chased anyone down and tried to suck blood," Susan concluded matter-of-factly.

Liffey did not know what to say. "Susan, do *you* think that this vampire thing is for real? What did it look like?"

Liffey tried to look reserved and skeptical—not

as totally thrilled as she actually was at the prospect of maybe solving a vampire mystery someday. She had never thought about vampires literally existing before, even though she had experienced something equally bizarre and hard to believe some years ago at the Halloween Feis in Seattle.

"Well, *something* must have happened! People said it was over six feet tall and had a pale, unearthly face and it wore a long black cape," Susan said. "Regular vampire attire."

"Then the sightings just *stopped* after 2008?" Liffey pressed for more details.

"So far, yes. But there was a long time between the first sighting and the last one...so who knows? There are still mining tunnels running underneath Mineral Point that were never filled in. Maybe whatever IT is lives underground in one of them and will wake up and rise again."

Liffey had almost forgotten that she was waiting for a pasty and figgy hobbin when the waitress set both dishes down on the table in front of her.

She plunged her knife into her half-portion of the folded-over-pie-crusted-thing called a 'pasty.'

First though, she decided to have a go at the figgy hobbin, just to get it over with.

Liffey had never much liked Fig Newtons, so she was very surprised when, after she had swallowed the first bite of figgy hobbin, she did not taste any figs. There were only regular raisins in a pastry exploding with caramel and cinnamon, topped with whipped cream.

"*This* is figgy hobbin?" Liffey was very sorry now that she had been so reluctant to taste it.

"It's incredible!"

Susan smiled knowingly.

CHAPTER SIX
November 1, 1842
The Long Walk Home

Jane opened her eyes when she could no longer hear the measured clacking of the horses' hooves making their way to the cemetery.

Patrick stood listlessly next to her, head hung low with shame, tears dripping from his chin, curly hair matted around his face like a baby's bonnet.

She placed her soft hand in his large, leathery one, and gently began leading him up High Street through the now somber crowd.

By the look of things, it appeared that the party atmosphere in Mineral Point had quickly faded. The church biddies had rushed off, leaving their picnic lunch behind and many of the spectators looked ill.

"I am so sorry, Jane," was all that Patrick could manage to say.

"I forgive you, Brother," Jane answered quietly. "Let's go home. I promise I won't welsh on you to Mam and Da but I wish I could bring that howling hound home with us so I could comfort it some."

"I think it probably belonged to Mr. Caffee," Jane said."Mam told me stories once about Mr. Hillas's black dog back in County Sligo and how it stood keening at his master's gate for a hundred years after Mr. Hillas was killed in a duel."

Patrick smiled. His little sister always embellished a story a bit. She was a good storyteller, like Mam. He wiped his tear-stained face with his sleeve.

Why had he ever thought that going to witness a public hanging would be entertaining?

It was the worst thing he had ever seen in his life, and he had forced his little sister to come with him.

Hoping to spare her grieving brother from being ridiculed by some of his loutish school friends in the crowd, Jane detoured off High Street through mostly empty back yards and alleys until they reached the outskirts of town.

Finally, Jane paused to catch her breath and wipe the sweat off her forehead. She tried not to think about how angry Mam was going to be when she saw what had happened to her new dress, now covered with dirt and corn stains which looked like they were permanently glued to the bottom of the skirt.

Patrick stared vacantly off into the distance.

"We had better keep moving," Jane said, looking west. "The sun is low in the sky and it'll start getting dark anytime now."

Patrick knew what she was thinking. "And we do not want to hear them wolves starting up with their yelping in the fields before we reach the farm," he said, finishing her sentence.

Jane did not point out that in his haste leaving the house earlier today, Patrick had not only neglected to bring along water and a lunch to give them some much needed energy for their long trek home, but he had also left the family's musket in its holder by the front door.

They would be completely defenseless if a pack of hungry wolves surrounded them out in the open.

If Jane were to be honest with herself, she would have to admit that she was much more afraid of Mrs. Gibbons' vicious barnyard chickens—especially the mean black rooster, than she was of any wolves.

That old black rooster had chased her many times when she was walking home from school and she had recurring nightmares about it lunging at her with its long, sharp beak.

They would pass by the Gibbons' farm on their way home today unless they took the shortcut again through the Widow's rotting cornfields like they had on the way to the hanging.

Jane was fairly certain that her brother would not want to do the Widow Hood's cornfields again. His memory of dragging her through them earlier today would be painful for him now.

Oh well. Mam told me that old gun had never been fired

and Da says wolves don't bother much with people.

Jane smiled to herself, thinking that her da was likely the only Irishman in the Territory that hunted with his bow and arrows.

CHAPTER SEVEN
So Much For Tranquility

After Liffey had wolfed down the last morsel of her new favorite desert, she turned her attention to the strange codicil Susan's uncle had added to his Last Will and Testament the week before he died.

Susan had left, promising she would come back to the Red Rooster after she went to check up on her father who was recuperating at home after a serious operation.

Liffey was secretly happy that she would be able to examine the codicil, with its sing-songy poems and bizarre cartoons, by herself.

She had always enjoyed figuring out rebus puzzles and anagrams and any other kind of brain teaser that came her way, but she had never seen anything like this codicil before. It appeared to be a hodgepodge-kind-of-puzzle which meant that it might be difficult to solve.

"When the Gray Dog barks" could be referring to the gray dog across the street. *Maybe the gold mine is located in the direction the dog is facing?* she thought. *But so what?*

Liffey moved on to the rooster. The irony of presently being in the Red Rooster Café looking at this document did not escape her. *So—what do roosters crow about? They announce the dawn? Or danger? Or they're hungry? Or scared?*

Liffey was becoming very discouraged because so

far, her ideas had been on the Kindergarten level.

The Chinese words must mean something important. I need to paste them on to a translation site. I am certain that the last symbol is not Chinese. It's definitely the symbol for the British pound. The men in bowler hats look like a group of snooty Mr. Banks from Mary Poppins. Are they bankers?

Also, was it only a strange coincidence that the gray pointer dog across the street had started howling when she passed under it and now she was looking at a cartoon of it?

Liffey tried to leave the 'unexplainable' things in her life out of the realm of the supernatural, but the howling wind had sounded exactly like an unearthly dog in distress. And the only dog around had been the gray metal one sitting on its platform above the sidewalk.

There was also the matter of all the unexplainable shadows—a solitary moving dog, the moving dog's shadow walking with the shadow of a tall man, a spinning rooster that morphed into a wagging dog's tail, a disembodied arm opening the Red Rooster's front door for her and then the same arm heading downhill with the wagging tail.

She was thankful that the red rooster on the sign had not crowed at her outside its café.

Before she could finish filing and sorting out all the jumbled-up thoughts racing around in her head, there was a kind of jerking back and forth inside her brain, like the sensation she always experienced when her Aunt Jean was braking hard at a stop sign and yelled: "Hold on, Liffey!"

An overwhelming need to make a copy of the codicil suddenly came over Liffey and she promptly began taking pictures of each page with her phone camera.

She had no idea why it had seemed so urgent to do this, but when she checked her 'In Box' and saw that she had successfully e-mailed all four codicil pages to herself, she breathed a sigh of relief and turned her attention back to deciphering the puzzle.

It was very nice to be working with someone for a change. She hoped she would not disappoint Susan. So far she was drawing a complete blank.

Someday, she might tell her new friend about her life-to-date. Then again, she might not.

Besides, like the almost unbelievable vampire story Susan had told her, who would ever really believe that so much could have already happened to a just-turned-14-year-old-girl who had recently moved to Mineral Point, Wisconsin?

Liffey was preoccupied, thinking about a vampire creeping around underneath Mineral Point in an abandoned mine tunnel, when Susan texted that her dad was not doing well and she needed to stay at home with him until her mother returned from work.

Liffey answered that she would stop by with the codicil as soon as she got up her nerve to take on the uphill trek through the snowstorm.

Even though Liffey had already successfully e-mailed the codicil to herself, she was used to getting fast curve balls thrown at her, so she sent it a second time, 'just in case,' to Facebook Messages for back-up. Next, she carefully folded the document and tucked it into a deep pocket inside her bulky parka along with her phone.

Outside looked like the North Pole when Liffey left the Rooster. She hunched over and began to make her way slowly uphill with the wind smacking at her back.

"Susan, Uncle Tom is here looking for our copy of Uncle William's codicil because his wife accidentally put theirs in the recyclables and he wants to make another copy. Can you imagine recycling a will with directions to a gold mine?" Susan could tell that her father looked uneasy.

She glanced over at her gloomy Uncle Tom who stood brooding next to her father's easy chair. He wore his usual sullen face and stared past Susan like she was not in the room.

In back of her father, in the small family room that also served as a home office, Susan could see that there were papers scattered over her mother's fragile Maplewood antique desk. It occurred to her that her Uncle Tom might have already been looking for the codicil while her father had been dozing.

Had he been planning to steal it while her father was sleeping? She decided not to ask any questions now, however, because her uncle had a wild, almost demented look on his normally expressionless face.

"No Pops, I don't have it on me. I left it with Liffey Rivers at the Rooster. She texted me that she'll bring it back here later, after the snow lets up some."

"Why in the world would you do that, Susan? What is wrong with you?" her uncle shouted angrily, shocking both Susan and her father with his hostile, aggressive tone.

"You don't want to be just giving away directions to our family's gold mine to everybody in Mineral Point!"

"I have to agree with your Uncle Tom, Susan. We probably should try to be careful," Susan's father said faintly, futilely trying to smooth over his older brother's crass, rough comments. Susan thought she detected apprehension and possibly even fear on her father's weary face and she decided at that moment that she was not going to let her father's obtuse older brother bully him anymore today, or for that matter, ever again.

She began to speak slowly, purposely using her childhood nickname for her uncle which he had always hated: "First, Uncle Tommy Tom, I do not think that my friend Liffey is exactly 'everybody in the Point,' and I would hardly call Uncle William's crazy codicil, a map to a gold mine! Liffey's trying to help us make sense out of it."

Susan paused to remove two pills from the bottle on the end table next to her father and handed them to him with a glass of water.

"Secondly, seriously? Mary Osborn says her aunt

said that Liffey Rivers' family is quite possibly the wealthiest family in the entire State of Wisconsin."

Tom Scott, very much taken aback by his niece's unusual impertinence, grunted and walked out of the house without saying goodbye.

Harry Scott smiled sheepishly. "I'm so sorry, Susan. I did not mean to sound critical and wimpy. I've spent my whole adult life trying to be nice to that ogre brother of mine, trying to keep him at bay like the mean dog he has always shown himself to be. I feel helpless not being able to earn a living. It puts a lot of stress on you and your mom."

"What stress? I'm not stressing out at all, Pops. We have everything we need and I can't really explain it, but I have a feeling that Liffey is actually going to be of some help to us."

Mr. Scott began to open his mouth but before he could reply to his daughter's kind words, his glasses slid down his nose and he began to snore quietly in his comfortable reclining chair.

But instead of easing gently into a late afternoon nap, Harry was jolted awake.

He had known the first time he looked at it that his uncle's codicil was two-pronged.

It was certainly a genuine puzzle leading to some kind of a gold mine which probably did exist—his uncle did not have a mean sense of humor. However, he strongly suspected that this codicil also contained private messages for FBI agent, Harry Scott, aka

'Gray Dog.'

He had always thought that Uncle William's code name within the CIA was 'Red Rooster' because his uncle would often crow at him when he was a little boy and regularly took him to the Red Rooster Café for what he called 'spy' food.

Years ago, when his uncle disappeared without explanation for several years, Harry had used his FBI intelligence sources throughout Asia and discovered that his uncle was in northeastern China, posing as a British minister called Henry Harper.

When William Scott had finally come back to Wisconsin, he never revealed to his nephew exactly what it was that he had been working on in China during those years. Probably because he knew Harry would not be safe if he had. He had hinted that it involved printing counterfeit British pounds on a massive scale and that he might have to call on Harry one day if he needed assistance.

Harry fought back tears of frustration. He was too sick to undertake interpreting his uncle's codicil riddle but he knew he had to try for his family's sake.

If he could summon up enough strength and mental acuity to examine the document competently, perhaps he would be able to make sense out of it.

One thing was already crystal clear to him. The codicil's multi-layered puzzle concerned something the Gray Dog needed to bark about and his Uncle William, the Red Rooster, was crowing at him, urging him to do the barking. The gold mine was secondary.

The man operating a large snowplow attached to a white pickup truck, drove slowly down High Street looking for the girl.

It was difficult to see through the gusting snow whether or not there was anyone walking on either side of the street. If he had to, he would ditch the truck and look for her inside the Red Rooster on foot after he made a second pass with the truck, driving uphill.

Today's snow storm had prevented most of Mineral Point's businesses from opening and it had been 'easy in' and an 'easier out' of the law office where his uncle's files were kept in old fashioned metal filing cabinets with alphabetized plastic labels. It had taken him no more than five minutes to search the 'S' folders, remove the William Scott files, and exit through the back door.

He had been told not to search the law office's computer files because hackers had already come and gone through cyberspace doors and had removed any trace of his uncle's codicil.

Tom had also visited his brother Dick's house earlier in the day and while Dick was in the kitchen preparing coffee for his unexpected morning guest, Tom had quickly removed his brother's codicil copy from the wall safe which he knew had been unlocked for the past twenty-five years.

As soon as he got his hands on Harry's copy, he

would hand over all three documents and collect the 250,000 British pounds promised by the anonymous man who had phoned him this morning.

Why someone would want to pay him so much for his uncle's practical joke codicils, was of no interest to him. He would leave the codicils at a dead drop in Mineral Point which would be revealed to him later today. He had already received 500 pounds earnest money in an envelope that someone had placed on the seat of his white pickup truck.

Liffey was relieved that the rooster on the sign above her stayed up on its perch this time and did not cast another eerie shadow that might turn into a dog's tail.

She considered the possibility that maybe she had finally had the 'big breakdown.' The one that her Aunt Jean was always warning her about. Her aunt had told Liffey many times that when things become so crazy and stressful that you cannot deal with them anymore, your brain starts to shut down without any advance warning and eventually tunes out completely. When that happens, you retreat into daydreams and endless babbling.

Aunt Jean definitely retreated long ago, Liffey thought, struggling to control the disordered thoughts racing around in her head.

Did I really see the shadow of the gray dog and then the rooster's tail turning into a wagging dog's tail? Or am I now as crazy as my Aunt Jean?

Liffey had decided to stay on the Red Rooster

side of the street to avoid walking under the pointer dog again, when a white pick-up truck with a huge snowplow on the front of it, came up from behind, drove up on the sidewalk and deliberately dumped a huge pile of snow in her path.

The truck then began backing up, barely missing Liffey as she flattened herself against a brick wall to avoid being run over. It traveled back out on to High Street again and stopped, facing uphill, in the wrong driving lane.

"Hello there!" A grubby-looking man that she had never seen before was leaning out of the white truck's driver's window.

"You're Susan's friend aren't you? She said you would probably be walking up High Street now and could probably use a ride."

Liffey almost acknowledged that she did know Susan, but when her body began to feel like there were a thousand red ants running up and down it, she instead heard herself lying: "No thanks. I don't mind walking and I don't know any Susan."

Liffey had no idea why she had just willfully lied about not knowing Susan, but she did know she needed to get out of there immediately.

How can this day be getting worse? Liffey thought.

She began walking backwards, keeping an eye on the truck, trying not to slip and fall. When the truck began to slowly move down the hill after her, Liffey compensated by tearing across the street and making her way uphill for half a block until she reached the

Gray Dog Deli.

Before the truck could get enough traction on the slippery road to follow her, Liffey reached the Gray Dog and ran inside.

Thank God for Velcro, she thought, ripping her feather-filled, over-sized parka open and reaching for the phone tucked in an inside pocket. She tried not to sound as pathetic and desperate as she actually felt when Maeve Rivers answered her call.

"Mom, I'm at the Gray Dog and I need you here right now! A man is stalking me outside in a white pickup truck."

After a split-second pause, Maeve said, "Lock the front door and then immediately go in back and hide. I'm only two minutes away and I'm already out the front door, calling the police. Tell the staff."

What staff?

There was no one in here. The Gray Dog was obviously not open. Someone had apparently left the front door unlocked by mistake.

Surely that man is not going to come in here after me?

Liffey called out: "Anybody here?"

All at once, she remembered her mother telling her to hide and barely managed to slip into a storage closet behind the food counter when the front door bell sounded with a friendly tinkle.

How could I have forgotten to lock the front door?

Her heart felt like it was doing a fast treble jig. She was afraid to breathe in or out while she listened to heavy boots stomping off snow as they slowly walked around, taking stock of the 'empty' premises.

The boots stopped. He must know where she was! Liffey groped around in the dark, unsuccessfully searching for a heavy object, waiting for the man to come to the closet, open the door and find her hiding inside.

The boots remained stationary until, after what seemed like at least a year had passed, another tinkle sounded and Liffey could see through a large crack in the door that Maeve Rivers had walked in, holding her hand in her purse.

She's got her pepper spray! Liffey thought, impressed with her mother's preparedness.

Before Maeve could verbally confront the man, he whipped around and rushed out the door.

"Liffey, you can come out now, honey, he's gone. I called the police again with the truck's license plate and I got a photo of the man from behind."

Liffey could breathe again. How had she ever managed to get by for so many years without this awesome mother? Tears of relief filled her eyes as she hugged Maeve Rivers close.

When an irritable, balding, middle-aged policeman arrived at the Gray Dog, he said that he was the lucky part time cop-sub filling in at the Point today during this "freakin blizzard with cars sliding off the road everywhere you looked and the police station's phone ringing off its hook."

He informed them that the Chief of Police and

all of the other regular officers were in Minneapolis attending a law enforcement seminar. "However, I let the snow messages pile up at the front desk while I ran the license plate you gave me, Mrs. Rivers, and then made some inquiries. The man in question is Tom Scott, and word around town has it that he's a decent man who has lived here in the Point his whole life."

"Since I live in Platteville, I have no opinion as to his character—good or bad. Anyway, I also called Mr. Scott to hear his take on things."

The temporary officer covered his mouth, yawed and turned his attention to Liffey. "You may call me Officer Sub," he said, attempting to be funny.

"Now, what made you think that this Mr. Tom Scott was a threat to your person, young lady?" he asked, stifling another yawn. Before Liffey could answer, Officer Sub went on, "Tom Scott told me that he was only trying to offer you a ride to his niece's house, to spare you from all the walking uphill through this blizzard, but you ran away from him."

Liffey resisted the impulse to snap back at him. *Ever hear the one about how you are like* **NEVER** *supposed to get into a stranger's vehicle, Officer Sub?*

Instead, irritated at having been called "young lady" by this obviously out-of-sorts policeman, who was obviously disinterested in her state-of-mind, she answered politely, with a hint of sarcasm: "I guess I need to learn how to relax and enjoy how safe I am here in Mineral Point, Officer Sub. I'm very sorry for the false alarm. I'm just not used to a strange man deliberately dumping snow in front of me to block my path, and then, after almost killing me with his truck on the sidewalk, offering me a ride and *then* stalking me when I say 'no thanks.' "

"Well then, I'm glad this has had a happy ending, young lady," Officer Sub said, smiling absently.

Liffey opened her mouth to reply but before she could say a word, she felt her mother elbowing her in the side, so she replied, "Me too, Officer Sub."

"Oh my, I don't believe I know your real name," Liffey gushed, "thanks ever so much for all your help, you're great!"

"Have a wonderful day," he said.

Liffey gritted her teeth as she watched Officer Sub waddle out of the Gray Dog Deli. The tinkle of the bell as the door opened made her wince a bit. She could never understand why adults always referred to her as "young lady." She didn't refer to them as "old man," or "old lady."

"Before we leave," Maeve began, "let's sit down for a bit and have some of that lovely carrot cake I see waiting for us over on the counter, Liffey. You deserve a reward for self-control and bravery. What an *awful* man! I'll tape a note with the money on top of the cake dome."

"Oh. And not to worry. While you were chatting away with Officer Sub, I called the Police Chief on his personal phone and he promised to get the High Street video footage of Mr. Scott's allegedly innocent offer to take you back to Susan's house, as soon as he returns."

"Video? Nobody was out there today on High Street recording anything, Mother."

"No one ever told you that there is a live camera fastened on the side of a building less than a block up from the Red Rooster?"

"No. Why would anyone want to do that? Is it like a security surveillance thing?" Liffey asked.

"No. It's a tourist thing. A 'live' camera is maybe exciting, I guess? At least to kids. You can get on the Point's Chamber of Commerce site and watch the action if you have nothing better to do. It only covers about a block."

"But, from what you have told me, it's the same block where the white truck made its threatening moves," Maeve replied.

"Well that's cool. Maybe there will be something helpful on the tape…" Liffey yawned like Officer Sub.

"When your father gets back next week from South Africa, I'll let him ask Tom Scott to explain his outrageous behavior. Attorney Rivers is, as we both know all too well, an expert cross-examiner. Tom Scott will be blabbering everything by the time your father is done with him."

"He'll stay away now that the police have him on record as harassing you. If he tries anything else, he will have to deal with me," Maeve said angrily, "because I am not letting you out of my sight."

"I am going to meet up with the Chief tomorrow when he gets back from Minnesota and if that video tape is incriminating..."

"Do you think I should tell Susan what her uncle did today?" Liffey asked, thoroughly enjoying her last bite of the carrot cake—her second amazing dessert of the day.

Maeve replied without a second thought.

"Absolutely, Liffey! She needs to know what her despicable uncle might be capable of doing next."

Liffey exhaled loudly.

So much for Mineral Point's tranquility.

CHAPTER EIGHT
A Blackening

For the second time that day, Jane made the sign of the cross as they passed by the lot where the first Catholic church in Mineral Point was slowly being built, stone by stone.

She prayed two prayers. One for forgiveness for William Caffee's sin. Then she asked for consolation for his broken-hearted companion. Jane knew in her own heart that the howling dog had belonged to Mr. Caffee and that it was inconsolable now.

Patrick had not yet composed himself. He had barely said anything by the time they had reached the border of Mineral Point. They moved slowly along, heading directly west into the burning orange light of the setting sun.

Jane was looking closely at the ground, checking for snakes, even though her da had told her that all the snakes living here in this part of the Wiskonsin Territory hibernated from mid-September until April because the autumn weather usually turned cold so early—sometimes even before the leaves had started to fall. Since today had been so warm, it occurred to Jane that the sleeping snakes might have emerged from their underground holes, thinking that it was already April.

Without having noticed when it happened, she realized that she no longer had to shield her eyes from the blinding sunlight that had been bothering her for the last half mile.

Shortly thereafter, an alarming blackness erased the fading sun on the horizon and a rumbling, barrel-rolling kind of din had started up. It seemed to Jane like everything was starting to vibrate.

Could this be Armageddon? Jane felt her head begin to swim and she began to tremble like she had at the hanging.

"Glory be to the Father and to the Son and to the Holy Ghost…" Jane began to pray, falling to her scrawny knees, flinching a bit when she felt one of the Widow Hood's foul corncobs, which a crow must have deposited on to the main road, seeping through her dress.

Patrick started to laugh, confirming what Jane

had already strongly suspected—that her brother had gone mad watching the gruesome execution unfold today.

What should they be doing now that the world could very well be ending? She fought back tears. She desperately longed for her mother—not her feeble-minded brother.

"For the love of our dear, sweet Savior, Patrick, we need to be praying now, not laughing like lunatics. Let's kneel down together right where we are and make our final confession. Mam says it is acceptable to God to confess our sins directly to Him if there is no priest available."

Jane was sick with fear, doing her best to appear calm for her nitwit brother's sake as she struggled to examine her conscience properly. Trying as hard as she was able, no sins came to mind. She could not think of one single sin that she had committed since the first, last and only time she had ever confessed them to Father Mazzuchelli.

She knew she had definitely committed a venial sin during that first confession, which, by the look of things now, might also have been her last confession to a priest, because she had made up all of the sins she had confessed. She had lied in the confessional so she would have something to say.

She prayed fervently under the blackened sky, that when Father Mazzuchelli had given her absolution for the sins she had invented, his blessing had also covered the sin about inventing those sins.

Mam called Father Mazzuchelli, 'Father Mathew Kelly' like all the other Irish did and said the poor priest had to travel 300 miles to St. Louis to confess his own sins to Bishop Loras.

Jane's mind was almost totally blank and all she could think of to pray was: *I am very sorry for everything that I cannot remember now that I have done to offend Thee, oh Lord. Please take me to heaven before the earth is consumed by flames and bless Mam and Da and my idiot brother Patrick who is now completely out of his sound mind and unable to confess his own sins.*

After Jane had completed her examination of conscience and asked for forgiveness, she recalled what Father Mazzuchelli had talked about once when he had shown up unexpectedly in Mineral Point from Dubuque. He preached that Sunday in his melodic Italian accent, wearing the lovely, silk-embroidered vestments he had brought over with him from Italy. Jane had thought at the time how nice it would be if she could have a dress made out of such exquisite material.

He had told his congregation how the Mesquakie Indians over by the Sinsinawa Mound, called this area "Manitoumie," which means "where the Great Spirit loves to dwell," because the land was so beautiful around here. This thought gave Jane great comfort now. If God actually lived around here, then maybe the end of the world would not be so bad.

Patrick was smiling broadly at her, like a fool, a stupid grin smeared on his face. When he started to laugh, Jane tried her best not to be distracted by her demented brother before she met her Maker

Patrick finally stopped laughing and pulled his sister back up on to her feet.

"Jane," he said, "the sky is black now because flocks of Passenger pigeons are blocking the sun! It ain't the end of the world, little nipper. Da said he heard in town last week that those pigeon birds were heading north, right up the Mississippi River, and we might hunt some if they stopped nearby to roost on this side of the river."

"There's miles and miles of them birds and if we was standing right underneath them now, I would be batting them birds down with both arms because Da said they get all stacked up on top of each other while they're flying and lots of 'em have to fly only a few feet above ground, because there ain't no space above them."

Jane felt relief pouring over her like warmed up bathwater.

"Passenger pigeons? I never heard Da talking about such birds, Patrick. But there is so little good meat here in Mineral Point, I imagine we could make us some good money if those birds did roost near us for awhile and you and Da got some."

"Men follow them pigeons, Jane, wherever they fly. They hold up long poles to knock 'em right out of the sky or stretch out fishing nets on low poles to tangle 'em up. And when the pigeons set down, men hunt them quicker than you and me when we go

69

gather up the eggs from underneath our hens."

"Pigeon birds ain't smart enough to escape and fly away when they are perched up in a tree neither," Patrick said. "They look those club men right in the eye before they get knocked down to the ground with one blow."

"And there ain't no need to worry ourselves about wolves anymore because all the wolves around here are thinking about having themselves some pigeon tonight," Patrick laughed.

It had been quite a day.

Moving briskly along under the pigeon-darkened sky, Jane thought about how anxious she was to slip out of her new dress, now soiled and stained, before Mam could look closely and see all the damage she had done to it.

She wondered if Passenger pigeon tasted much like chicken.

CHAPTER NINE
Dog, Rooster, Fox

Liffey took off her wet parka and hung it up on its hook in the entrance hallway. She reached into the deepest inside pocket where she had carefully placed Susan's uncle's codicil.

It was not there.

She checked all the inside and outside pockets.

Nothing. Just an old Kleenex and a 'To Do' list she had written over a year ago.

She did some slow breathing and again searched all six of the parka's pockets, inside and out.

Still nothing.

Confused and fearing the worst, she sat down on the couch directly in front of their stone fireplace, but the only thing burning inside her house now was her stomach, which felt like a volcano had erupted down there when she eventually realized what had to have happened.

The codicil must have fallen out of my coat pocket at the Gray Dog when I got my phone out to call Mother. HOW could I not have noticed? I should never have folded it up...

The realization that Susan's uncle had picked it up off the floor like she had personally handed it to him on a silver platter was shattering.

It was clear to Liffey now that Tom Scott had

been after the codicil all along—not her. And she had literally just given it to him. No wonder she had not heard him creeping around inside the Gray Dog searching for her while she had been hiding in the closet. He must have discovered the codicil almost immediately after coming inside and had exited the Deli as her mother was walking through the front door.

What if I had not e-mailed myself a copy? How could I have ever told Susan that I just LOST it?

Liffey knew that there had to be other copies—the Scott's lawyer would certainly have extras and Susan's other uncles each had one too. So why would Susan's creepy Uncle Tom be trying to confiscate his siblings' codicils if he already had one of his own? To make sure he had a head start looking for the gold mine because he had all of his brothers' copies?

Okay. This pity party is officially over now. Time to make new copies and get one over to Susan's house before her uncle makes another brilliant move.

She texted Susan: *Will bring codicil soon. Need to talk privately. Bringing my mom with me.*

While Liffey waited for her mother to call her father in Johannesburg to go over the unnerving events that had transpired in Mineral Point earlier in the day, she began to study the cartoons again.

There was something about a rooster and dog and fox that seemed almost ready to click on in her brain, if she could find the right button. It seemed familiar somehow. Like there was a story in her head waiting to be remembered.

Maeve reported from the library that she would be on the phone for some time yet: "Liffey, honey, I'm really sorry I'm talking so long with your father. He went to get some coffee. I promise I'll keep him away from you until tomorrow. You need some quiet time before he starts firing questions at you. He's already sputtering. Your brother is out with Sister Helen or I would put him on."

"No problemo," Liffey called back, enormously relieved that she was not going to have to field a barrage of questions about today being aimed at her. Her well-meaning, lawyer-father could be completely exhausting. Not to mention overbearing.

"Take all the time you need, Mom. I'm keeping myself occupied."

Liffey was focusing on the codicil's cartoons she had sent from her phone, when she felt a bolt of flash-from-the-past-lightning. Her mother's voice had activated a long-ago memory of an Aesop's Fable she had loved to have her parents read to her. The one about a dog, a rooster and a fox!

Liffey read through several online versions of the same Aesop's Fable and noted that there seemed to be recurring facts and the same moral in each of them.

One moonlight night a Fox was prowling about a farmer's hen-coop, and saw a Cock roosting high up beyond his reach.

"Good news, good news!"he cried.

"Why, what is that?" said the Rooster.

"King Lion has declared a universal truce. No beast may hurt a bird like you henceforth, but all shall dwell together in brotherly friendship."

"Why, that certainly is good news," the Rooster said; "and look there—I see someone coming, with whom we can share these good tidings." And so saying he craned his neck forward and looked into the distance.

"What is it you see?" said the Fox.

"It is only my master's Dog that is coming towards us. What, going so soon?" he continued, as the Fox began to turn away as soon as he had heard the news.

"Will you not stop and congratulate the Dog on the reign of universal peace?"

"I would gladly do so," said the Fox, "but I fear he may not have heard of King Lion's decree."

Moral: Cunning often outwits itself.

Liffey was stumped as to how this fable's moral might relate to the Scott's codicil and hoped Susan might have some ideas. It had to be the right story because it had a rooster, a fox and a dog.

Next, she went to an online translation service and pasted the Chinese writing above the cartoon of the crowing rooster on page two of the codicil. The translation from Chinese into English thrilled her:

Meatloaf to go or eat here every day.

Liffey felt like her head was going to explode with excitement. She knew *exactly* what this meant!

It had to be the Chinese-to-English translation of the Red Rooster's outdoor, totally boring pasty sign which, according to Susan, had said the exact same thing ever since she or anyone else in Mineral Point could remember:

PASTY DAILY
TO GO
OR EAT HERE

The crazy Codicil to William Scott's Last Will and Testament, was finally starting to make some sense to Liffey. Susan's odd uncle might very well be saying that the Red Rooster's outdoor sign contained a message about something other than just eating a pasty, or, like in Chinese, a "meatloaf."

The Rooster's hidden message on its sign might actually turn out to be her first real life anagram!

Liffey had learned how to solve anagrams years ago when she used to play 'spy' with her dad. He had patiently worked with her, using letters from their Scrabble game, until she was able to rearrange the letters in anagrams by herself to make other words and discover hidden messages.

He told her that being able to solve complicated anagrams was "step one" in becoming a real spy.

Liffey had been very proud the day her father had presented her with an **OFFICIAL SPY** certificate in a glass frame when she was ten years old. It was her reward for years of hard work.

Even though Liffey knew it was totally lame, her 'Official Spy" certificate had hung on her bedroom wall ever since.

But why is the Rooster's sign message written in Chinese?

And why is there the £ sign for British pounds sterling blended into the Chinese message?

There has to be a reason.

CHAPTER TEN
The Return of Aunt Jean

Jean Rivers had to postpone her move to Mineral Point because of a freak snowstorm. This irritated her greatly because it had been almost impossible for her not to slip up and tell her family that she had sold her condo and purchased a lovely stone cottage just a few doors down from them.

Liffey would be thrilled to practice Irish dancing steps with her again and her sister-in-law, Maeve, would mold both Liffey and herself into champion Irish dancers in no time at all.

Just look at what Maeve had already done for her daughter! Not to mention Liffey's Irish girlfriend, Sinead McGowan. The two of them had absolutely triumphed at the Anchorage Feis.

Maeve Rivers would be ecstatic when she found out that she was going to be the TCRG at Mineral Point's first Academy of Irish Dance. Maeve had told her that she had been one of those four-lettered-T-people some years before Liffey was born.

Apparently, Irish dance schools needed to have a TCRG—whatever that meant, if their students were going to be able to compete at feiseanna.

Why the Irish dancing community insisted on calling an Irish dance competition a 'feis,' she would never understand.

Why feis judges had to have an Attention Deficit diagnosis in order to get their ADCRG feis-judging credentials was totally beyond her as well. *I suppose if feis judges were able to pay close attention, they would not be able to last much more than twenty minutes at a feis,* Jean reasoned.

When Jean had thought to do an internet search for 'TCRG,' 'Terminal City Roller Girls,' was the only possible match. She supposed that if the TCRG were a male, it would probably stand for 'Terminal City Roller Guys,' which was all very confusing because Jean did not know that Irish dancers had the option of competing in roller skates. It must be restricted to places like Las Vegas or Nebraska.

John Bergman opened the letter he had received yesterday from his friend Liffey Rivers. She was the only person he had ever known who actually wrote letters in long-hand and they always smelled like lilacs.

He had hoped to surprise Liffey today by arriving with her Aunt Jean, who had asked him to come to Wisconsin to help her move to Mineral Point, but a snowstorm had shut down General Mitchell Airport in Milwaukee and Jean Rivers had to postpone her surprise move. She had rescheduled his flight from New Hampshire to the following day.

He had promised Liffey's aunt that he would not tell Liffey that he was coming to help for a few days over his fall break. Jean had decided that the weather would be fine the next day and had changed his flight to Madison, Wisconsin, where together they would drive the last 65 miles to Mineral Point.

Neil Rivers and Sister Helen, who had cared for him for years after he had been found abandoned in a baby stroller in the Sisters' chapel at the Holy Infant Home For Disabled Children, spent the day on a field trip that his father, Robert Rivers, had arranged for the older children—a trek to watch the famous South African Lipizzaner horses perform four-footed ballets and precision maneuvers.

After a pleasant day, Neil realized that, other than Sister Helen, the only thing he really missed now that he had moved to the United States to live with his family, were the Jungle Oats he used to eat every morning for breakfast while Sister Helen tutored him in German and French grammar.

When Sister Helen told him that there was a freak snowstorm happening in the Midwest, Neil texted his older sister Liffey with a "*ha ha*" and sent a photo of himself outdoors, enjoying a beautiful, balmy day in the South African late spring.

He did not want to admit to anyone, especially his older sister, that he would give anything to be in that freak snow storm himself right now, and could barely contain himself waiting for what he hoped would be a record snowfall in Wisconsin this winter.

He had never seen real snow until Sister Helen brought him to be reunited with his family on an

Alaskan cruise ship. Sister told him that there had only been 22 days of snow over the last 100 years in Johannesburg. He wanted at least 100 days of snow every year in Wisconsin.

Neil had nightmares about black mamba snakes and saving his sister's life. Against all odds, after the mamba had bitten him on both legs, he had survived and learned to walk for the first time.

Sister Helen thought that the neurotoxins from the mamba's venom may have actually helped him regain the use of his leg muscles.

She said it was a real "miracle."

CHAPTER ELEVEN
Fables and Spies

After Susan had gotten Maeve up to speed as to Harry's weakened condition, she went off to her bedroom with Liffey to find out firsthand what her Uncle Tom had been up to earlier in the day.

Maeve saw Harry seemed to be sleeping fitfully in his recliner and went into the kitchen to pre-heat the stove for dinner.

Susan's mother called to say she was still trapped in Dodgeville and would come home when the roads were plowed. Maeve assured her everything was fine here and to spend the night at the hospital if she needed to.

Harry Scott began to babble loudly in his sleep. Maeve hesitated to tune in, even though she did not think that listening to someone talking gibberish could technically be considered eavesdropping.

However, when he suddenly became extremely agitated and began shouting: "Red Rooster crowed! Gray Dog must bark! Stop Fox! Find. Too late," she began to listen intently.

When Harry began speaking Mandarin Chinese, which Maeve only recognized because she had spent a long-ago college semester in China studying Tang Dynasty architecture, she became truly concerned.

There were Chinese words in the codicil directly above the crowing rooster cartoon and below it, a fox riding on a horse chasing a man. There was also a gray dog barking rhyme before the rooster page. *Harry must be stressing out over his uncle's codicil*, Maeve thought.

Was the codicil about more than a treasure hunt and an Aesop's Fable with a moral aimed at William Scott's three nephews? Liffey had suggested this very possibility on their way over here.

Before Maeve told Liffey that she had seen Tom Scott reading something when she had entered the Gray Dog Deli, Liffey told her that she had already figured out that what Tom Scott had really been after was the codicil, not her.

Maeve was preoccupied with trying to figure out *why* Tom Scott had been chasing after her daughter in the middle of a blizzard. Why such urgency? Susan had told her uncle that she had left the codicil at the Red Rooster with Liffey and that Liffey would bring it back to the Scott's house. Apparently, that had not been good enough for him and he had behaved like he was on some sort of 'commando mission.'

If he was out to destroy all the codicil copies so that he would be the only nephew with access to it, then it made sense—he was greedy. He wanted the gold. However, unless he was totally technologically impaired, he would have to suspect that there could easily be an unlimited number of codicils available on computers by now.

Maybe it had even been tweeted about in some circles.

Maeve was putting vegetable lasagna in the oven when another thought occurred to her. *Maybe Tom Scott will think that he needs to get the hard drive on Susan's computer.*

If someone else had dispatched Tom to collect his siblings' codicil copies, for whatever reason, then that person might also have the ability to hack into online and hard drive files pertaining to the codicil—like the message Susan had texted Liffey yesterday.

But Tom Scott would not know any of this. He was probably computer illiterate and might think he needed to steal Susan's computer. And what about the family lawyer? Had Tom already broken into that law office and stolen the Scott family's files?

Maeve was not particularly worried about Liffey's security having been compromised. Liffey's phone and computer were both ultra protected. Liffey's e-mails were completely secure on both ends but Susan Scott's files would probably not be so safe.

Unless Maeve was very wrong, they could expect another visit from Uncle Tom shortly, under some pretense other than removing the Scotts' computer. She strongly suspected that he was not working alone and Susan had revealed that she thought that her uncle was not smart enough to have his own agenda.

Before Maeve had time to check on dinner, or contact her husband, Robert, about Harry's ominous blathering, there was a loud pounding on the door and Tom Scott swaggered in.

"Well, well, looky here. I was all worried about you Harry, what with Ann all trapped at the hospital and everything but it looks like you already have another pretty lady taking care of you."

Harry remained sleeping.

"Where's my niece? Where's Susan?" he slurred as Maeve approached him. "I need to ask her some questions."

"Susan is very busy," Maeve replied, trying not to show how angry she was that her psychic flash had materialized.

She was relieved that Susan's slovenly uncle did not seem to recognize her from the Gray Dog Deli earlier that day. She had been wearing sunglasses and a faux fur hat, and he had been preoccupied looking at the codicil Liffey had dropped.

Don't push your luck, Uncle Tom, she thought.

"How did you know that Ann was stuck at the hospital?" *Surely their house phone cannot be tapped? Who would want to do something like that?*

Tom caught her suspicious vibe and pushed past her, moving towards Susan's bedroom.

"I already told you that Susan is busy and I am asking you to leave this house immediately!" Maeve roared, following closely behind the tall, stocky man as she dialed 911 and removed a small canister of pepper spray from her purse.

She aimed the nozzle and waited.

CHAPTER TWELVE
Pending Revelation

By the time Jane and Patrick spotted the outline of their large, half-timbered farmhouse in the clearing, a natural darkness covered the earth. A full harvest moon had risen in the sky, indicating that the migratory pigeons had either landed or flown farther north.

So far, there had been no wolves howling in the fields and Mrs. Gibbons' chickens had mercifully remained in their coops.

Patrick hoped that his parents had returned from their shopping trip by now so that he and his father might be able to set off as soon as possible to hunt pigeons.

Brother and sister halted outside the gate when they saw that there were two horses tied to the posts in front of the house. There were also two large men sitting on the porch glider swing like they belonged on the premises.

"Patrick, what should we do now? Should we hide from them? What if they have already hurt Mam and Da?" Jane whispered apprehensively.

Patrick scrutinized the situation and saw that the door to the small carriage barn stood open. He could see that it was empty, so their parents had not yet returned.

Deciding that it was time he stepped up and took care of his little sister for a change, he said: "You go to your hiding spot, Jane. I'll talk with these men. They probably mean no harm. Mam and Da ain't back yet; the carriage barn door is wide open."

"I don't think I should leave you alone, Patrick," Jane said bravely. "What if they just shoot you right off?"

"Well then, that'll be that I reckon. What good would it do if they shoot both of us right off?"

"No, Jane," Patrick continued, "you go hide and if you hear some shots, sneak over to the road the back way and watch for Da and Mam to warn them. I'm going to walk right up to them strangers and ask what business they have here."

Jane, for the third time today, was overtaken by fear as she obeyed her brother's command. He was right. She would be of no real use to Patrick under these circumstances and might make things worse.

"How, in the name of all that is holy, could it have taken anyone so long to make their way back to their own wagon?" Catherine Scott complained bitterly, as the Scott's wagon turned right on the final stretch of road before they reached home.

"It was a terrible, shameful thing, being part of that lynch mob, Paul. And then, losing our way and walking around in circles searching for our patient horse after the hanging."

"I will never understand why you insisted we go to that lynching in the first place. I have never known you to be a shallow man who takes pleasure in such gruesome goings-on as you watched today."

"I promise that I will explain it to you in good time," Paul answered quietly. "And it was no lynching, Catherine. It was a court-ordered, legal execution."

"You lied to me, Paul! You told me we were off to be shopping in Dodgeville and the next thing I know, are you not turning off from the main road and heading down into Mineral Point the back way. You are a sneaky man, Paul Scott."

"If anyone from church saw us there today, we will probably be excommunicated! Philistines is what we became today, Paul. Both of us were Philistines. May God have mercy on our souls."

"Catherine, you never opened your eyes. Not once. Did you not pray for William Caffee's soul, begging God for mercy and did you not fast all day for the condemned man? Here, eat this piece of bread before you expire along with him."

Catherine accepted the bread and said, "My poor little Jane is probably half mad by now being without me when the sun left the sky and darkness covered the earth. It was surely a sign from heaven, Paul, and our children were alone walking home from school when it happened! What must they think of us? Not hitching up the horse and going for them on the road when it looked like the very end of the world?"

"And if you tell me one more time it was pigeons blotting out the setting sun and not the hand of God pointing towards our shameful wickedness, I will not be responsible for my actions, Paul Scott."

Paul did not reply. He knew when there was nothing more he could say to appease his wife. Later on, he would get up his nerve and tell Catherine the real reason they had made the trip to see William Caffee hang.

"Humpf," Catherine snorted.

"Pigeons indeed!"

CHAPTER THIRTEEN
Evacuation

Tom Scott dropped quickly down to the floor and rolled on to his stomach, futilely trying to escape from the pepper spray floating around him like an early morning mist. He was calling Maeve Rivers names that Liffey would have to ask someone about later because she had no idea what they meant.

Tears flowed down his face and he coughed and choked while Maeve stood guard over him, unmoved by his litany of grievances and insults.

When he had started to kick in Susan's bedroom door, Maeve realized that he was either a man on a some sort of sinister errand, very drunk, drugged, or completely insane and was not going to politely leave the premises as she had ordered him to do.

She hoped that the police would arrive quickly, remove Tom Scott, and keep him at the local jail until she had a chance to discuss all that had happened so far with the Police Chief tomorrow.

She worried about Harry Scott in the next room who had miraculously slept through the noisy, ugly confrontation. Slowly recovering from surgery, he did not need this upsetting family drama.

Maeve's mind was in high gear.

It was hard to believe that the sniveling Tom Scott on the floor in front of her could be involved alone in the gathering up of William Scott's codicil copies. She was very worried that perhaps the person or people that wanted all the hard copies, might prefer a master guide to the codicil.

From what she had heard when Harry Scott had been sleep-ranting, *he* might very well be that guide.

Maeve knew that she needed to talk to her husband, Robert. He would have the contacts to run background checks at the deepest levels on Harry Scott and William Scott.

She had heard Harry say "Gray Dog" and "Red Rooster" and speaking in Chinese. Maybe one name, or both, would turn up in intelligence files shared by Interpol. Perhaps it was significant that Harry knew Mandarin Chinese.

She sent a *'help needed asap'* text to her husband in Africa, relating as much as she could recall about everything Harry Scott had said in his sleep.

A loud knocking on the door erupted and two police officers entered with guns drawn.

Maeve was dismayed to see that Officer Sub was still on duty and studying his arrogant body language, was probably the officer in charge here. The much younger trainee officer appeared to be apprehensive and inexperienced.

This is just great, Maeve thought crossly.

"Well, here you are again, Mrs. Rivers. I was told that this was the Harry Scott residence," Officer Sub said, curling his lower lip.

"This is Harry Scott's house, Officer. Tom Scott barged in without permission and demanded to see his niece, Susan, who was in her bedroom. He began kicking at the door when Susan told him to go away."

"I see," said Officer Sub, glancing over at Harry Scott, who was sound asleep. "Looks to me like the man of this house didn't have much to say about calling in the police. But then, that seems to be your particular specialty, doesn't it Mrs. Rivers?"

Maeve bit her tongue and remained silent.

"Will you kindly fill me in as to why Mr. Tom Scott is moaning in pain over there on the floor, Mrs. Rivers? What did you do to him?"

"I pepper-sprayed him when he was trying to kick in Susan's bedroom door, Officer."

Susan emerged from her bedroom with Liffey and offered her version: "Liffey and I were terrified. He kept screaming at me to open the door and when I told him to go away, he started kicking at the door hard like he was trying to break it down."

"And just what do you expect me to do about this, Mrs. Rivers? He is the girl's uncle, correct?"

Maeve was having great difficulty understanding why Officer Sub was still unwilling to help her with this dangerous man.

Earlier today, he had treated her like *she* was the one out of line when she had reported Tom Scott's aberrant behavior towards her daughter on High Street.

Now, he acted like kicking in a door in someone else's house, terrorizing children, was just fine if you were related. What in the world was going on here?

Liffey, who was becoming increasingly agitated

and could no longer disregard the pins and needles slithering all over her torso, all at once blurted out: "Could you *please* just get Susan's uncle out of here, Officer Sub? Take him home, maybe? He's obviously having a bad day."

Maeve was shocked. It was not like her daughter to so rudely barge in like that.

Officer Sub nodded and smugly gestured at his assistant officer to come with him to help him pick up Tom Scott, who was still sobbing on the floor, blaming Maeve for her "unprovoked, vicious attack."

Maeve thought her daughter must have sensed something was going terribly wrong here to have said such a ridiculous thing to the police. But before she could sort things out with Liffey, she was interrupted by a message beep.

It was from Robert. His text said: *We have a global warming problem here in South Africa for both families and I'm sick of it, aren't you?*

Maeve felt her stomach flip-flop.

Her husband had just texted her in code that they were all in grave danger here and needed to get into their safe house as quickly as possible.

They needed to leave *now*.

How had Liffey known?

Without a parting word, Maeve opened the front door for Officer Sub and his companion officer as they helped Tom Scott out to their squad car.

Next, she hurried into the Scotts' spacious garage to heat up her van for Harry.

When Robert Rivers had purchased this custom designed van, which reminded her of an armored tank, she thought it was ridiculous.

Now she would need its lift ramp and the gurney attached to the wall of the van to move Harry Scott safely out of his house and into what had now become a flight vehicle.

Maeve unhitched the gurney, activated the lift, and walked quickly back into the house where the girls were back at studying the codicil. She tried to remain calm and said: "We have a global warming problem, Liffey and I'm just sick of it, aren't you?"

Liffey was speechless.

Her mother had just said in code, the dreaded words her father had made both of them memorize. Translated: "Danger drawing near. Go to safe house immediately. Say nothing."

"I beg your pardon, Mrs. Rivers, but what in the world are you talking about?" Susan asked anxiously when she saw the look on Liffey's face and Maeve pushing what looked like a stretcher on wheels.

Liffey shook her head and placed her 'hush' finger to her lips, sign language telling Susan not to say anything further.

Susan looked at Liffey with raised eyebrows.

Liffey returned her friend's look with a smile and said, "The Rivers family has always been green and concerned about increasing global warming, Susan."

Then she whispered, "Let's help my mother get us out of here and we will explain everything when we get to where we're going. It's a good thing you told us to park our van inside your garage, Susan, or we would all freeze to death trying to get Harry out of here."

Liffey and a wide-eyed Susan, covered up Harry with his black and red afghan, lifted him up gently from his reclining chair, on to the gurney, and pushed him out to the garage on to the van's lift platform.

Inside the van, they secured the gurney on the floor between two metal bars.

I never dreamed I would actually be doing this, Maeve thought shakily. *Thank you Robert for always being such a worry wort, super nerd. I only know what to do now because you made me pay attention.*

"Liffey, you told me that you sent Susan a copy of the codicil from your phone, right?" Maeve asked.

"Yes, mother, I'm afraid I did," Liffey replied.

"But like I've already told you, Susan sent me a text late last night about the codicil," Liffey said, retrieving her messages on her phone.

"Here it is: *Reminder. Lunch tomorrow at Rooster. Will bring Uncle William Scott's mystery codicil to his last will and testament. Puzzle fun with gray dog, red rooster, fox, horse cartoons. See u then. We will solve! Sleuth Scott.*"

"Okay, run and get the desk top computer then," Maeve instructed. "But first, send your father the codicil so he can get it to Interpol."

"Susan, grab any important family papers, if you know where they are kept. You have three minutes. Liffey, please help her."

Susan followed Liffey back into the house.

"Liffey, *what* is going on here?" Susan murmured fearfully. "Is my house going to explode?"

"Probably not. I think my mom is more worried about your dad being in a safe place," Liffey said as she forwarded the four pages of the codicil to her father.

"So, get a few family photos and some memory stuff and don't forget your uncle's cartoons," Liffey said, acutely aware of how frightened her friend must be.

Soon, a disoriented Susan, holding a small box of memories, joined Liffey, who was carrying the heavy desk top computer terminal out to the van where Maeve was waiting with the lift.

"We're going now, Susan. It's going to be okay and I promise that I will explain everything when we are back at our place out of this unending storm."

"But why would we be safer at your house, Mrs. Rivers? It's just a house like ours."

"I know, Susan. You'll see."

Maeve drove slowly down the driveway through slushy, melting snow drifts.

Golf ball sized hail began pelting the roof, but changed to freezing rain before their vehicle had reached the end of the driveway.

Forks of lightning stabbed the sky, followed by claps of loud thunder.

Liffey's eyes became saucer-like when she looked out the window.

The TV weatherman had gotten it all wrong this morning when he had said a 'Snowmageddon' was coming today.

This looked way more like an Armageddon—or whatever the end of the world was supposed to look like.

CHAPTER FOURTEEN
A Family Reunion

Patrick wanted to run and hide like Jane but he was determined to make up for having been the worst older brother in the entire history of the human race today by protecting his little sister now.

He prayed a quick *Ave* and stepped forward in plain view of the two men sitting on his porch.

"Hello there! Are you gentlemen lost? May I be of service to you?" he said with false bravado.

His heart was beating so rapidly he was afraid it might explode in his chest.

"That depends, son. We already helped ourselves to your well water for our horses but we are mightily hungry. Would your parents be coming back soon then? We would much appreciate staying in your hay barn tonight. We have had a long, hard day and a long ride ahead of us tomorrow morning."

Patrick thought that perhaps he had been too hasty with his offer to be of service because these men seemed to be very needy. He hoped they were not polite, dangerous thieves.

While he was struggling with how to answer the strangers' requests, he heard his parents arguing in their wagon a short distance away. He ran out into the road, waving his arms to signal them to stop.

"Da! We have company! Two drifters are sitting on our porch swing like they belong here." He hoped this would encourage his da to be on alert as to the best way to handle this threatening situation. The horse slowed its pace and finally came to a full stop on the road in front of the house.

The two intruders stepped down from the cedar wood glider and approached the wagon. "Is that you then, Cousin Paul?" one of them called out. "It's Levi and John."

Patrick was shocked. Da was their cousin? Why hadn't they told him this when he talked to them?

"Who are these cousins of yours then, Paul?" Catherine inquired quietly, studying them carefully as they drew closer.

"They are my Uncle James Caffee's sons. He and his wife, Elizabeth Scott, my aunt, died twenty some years ago, back in 1820, and left their sons, William, Levi and John orphaned. William was only eight-years-old when it happened. He was the oldest. The Scott side of the family took the lads in and raised them. I shot marbles with them at family gatherings."

"The man who was hanged today was my cousin William. I called him Billy. I lost touch with all three of my cousins after I went over to Sligo to live and met you, Catherine." Catherine swallowed hard, trying to process her husband's startling revelation.

Wait till Jane hears this, Patrick thought, looking to

see if she had ventured out of her tree house on the north side of the house. Patrick grinned. It was hard to figure how his sister actually believed that no one knew where she always went to hide.

From the darkness, a little girl's voice squeaked: "How do you do, cousins? I am Jane Scott and am pleased to make your acquaintance. Won't you join us inside and take some refreshment? You have had a hard day grieving for your brother and I would be honored to make you a supper to help comfort you."

Catherine, Paul and Patrick's mouths hung open as Jane came out from the shadows, linked arms with her new-found cousins, the remaining two Caffee brothers, and escorted them into the house.

Before dinner, Patrick was sitting on the porch alongside the other men, munching on apples and sipping tea with milk and sugar. He had forgotten all about begging his father to take him pigeon clubbing.

Jane, now a lady of the house along with her mother, helped prepare the large ham hanging in the smoke house they had been saving for a special occasion.

"Jane, would you kindly organize the parsnips and other vegetables for our supper? The root cellar is still full up," Catherine said.

Jane was ecstatic. She was being invited to select the other vegetables for tonight's dinner! Mam had never trusted her to undertake this important task before. It seemed that both she and her brother had grown up quite a lot today.

After the dinner table had been cleared, Jane was taken aback when her new cousins began moving the sturdy wooden dinner chairs that Da had built last year, out from the kitchen and into the front room, closer to the hearth.

Patrick and Jane stood up, puzzled, but too polite to make any enquiries as to what their cousins were doing. They watched silently as their parents joined the cousins, moving furniture around wordlessly, like they were all on some kind of organized team.

Levi Caffee left the room briefly and returned carrying a battered violin case. *Was he going to play music at a time like this?* Jane was horrified.

Mam got out the family rosary from where she kept it in the four drawer cupboard, second drawer down. To Jane's relief, they only recited the first five decades. She was far too stirred up to pray properly.

Da produced, seemingly out of nowhere, a clay pipe and a small dish of tobacco—and a fiddle!

Jane was astonished. *Am I after completely losing my mind? My da has never smoked nor played a fiddle!* She sat down next to her brother, completely bewildered.

Soon the fiddling began and to add to the Scott children's astonishment, their mam got up from the semi-circle of chairs and began to dance to the fiddle music.

She held her arms straight down at her sides. Only her feet were moving, pounding on the wooden floor like she was stomping out brush fires.

The fiddles picked up the tempo and soon Mam was flying all over the room, leaping and keeping rhythm with her feet to the music. When the fiddling stopped, Da and Mam recited together: "May the soul of William Caffee, through the mercy of God, rest in peace. Amen."

Levi and John talked some about their lives in Kentucky with their brother, William. Three sons had been born to Elizabeth Scott and James Caffee— William, Levi and John. Both parents had died in 1820 in a tragic accident and the boys had been raised by their mother's brother on his farm in Kentucky.

They had kept their family name, 'Caffee,' and William and Levi eventually headed to the lead mines in Southwestern Wisconsin. John had fought in the Blackhawk War and then married and settled down on a farm in Iowa.

William and Levi had lived over near Gratiot's Grove where they worked in one of Henry Gratiot's mines—until William shot Samuel Southwick.

"Will we ever be seeing the both of you again then, cousins?" Jane asked hopefully.

"I reckon not, Jane," Levi answered sadly.

"We would be much obliged though if you might visit the graveyard every now and then to tend to William's plot. There ain't no money for a proper stone or marker but he's at rest in the Potter's Field part of the public cemetery, back in the southwest corner where John and I buried him."

"I believe that he would much appreciate having

some company on November first each year," John Caffee added. "And if you see old Gray Dog about in town, maybe you might be bringing him home if your mam would allow it."

" 'Gray Dog' was the only name our brother ever called that animal. The poor mutt was sitting on the grave this afternoon right after Levi and me filled it in. I suppose Gray Dog is waiting for William to turn up again. Them two were inseparable," Levi said, wiping a few stray tears away from his eyes.

The Caffee brothers stood up and thanked their hosts, hugging Jane and Catherine, shaking hands solemnly with the men.

John and Levi walked slowly out to the hay barn. Paul Scott had already bedded down their horses and left warm blankets and pillows for his cousins.

Catherine invited them to a breakfast fry in the morning. But when she went out to the barn at first light the next day with cups of steaming tea for the Caffee men, they had already gone.

Just after dawn, Gray Dog's vigil at his master's grave was interrupted by James James, a local blacksmith and the only man in the vicinity known to have the same first and last name. He had with him a large beef bone to fortify the grieving animal. James James had promised William Caffee, as he cut the shackles from his wrists before the hanging, that he would look after his gray pointer dog and find a man who might be looking for a good hunting companion.

102

CHAPTER FIFTEEN
Intervention

Robert Rivers had detective Louise Anderson dispatched and on her way to Mineral Point, Wisconsin, an hour after contacting her office in Saint Louis.

Slightly correcting the pitch of the plane she was piloting, Louise circled and began her descent into Rockford International Airport.

She had received a life-changing phone call five minutes after her conversation with Attorney Rivers had ended. It was obvious that someone had tapped into the phone call he had made to her from South Africa. *Very sophisticated,* she thought, as the plane's wheels expertly touched down on the runway. *Who is monitoring Robert's phone calls?*

The snowstorm pummeling most of the Midwest had stopped at the Wisconsin border, leaving Illinois with dry roads and clear skies.

What was not clear to Louise now, was whether or not she should accept the enormous sum of money which would have already been delivered to a law firm in the Cayman Islands, to be held for her until she personally came to collect it.

Because of the snow, she had not been able to get clearance to land in either Madison, Wisconsin, or Dubuque, Iowa. She had reserved an all-wheel drive vehicle at the airport to get through the snowstorm in Wisconsin and would hopefully get to the Rivers family without ending up in a ditch.

First, she needed to pick up an 'Ann Scott' at a hospital in Dodgeville, Wisconsin, and drive both of them to Robert Rivers' safe house.

Second, she needed to decide whose side she was on.

As Maeve had requested, Robert Rivers asked his liaison at Interpol to run a global data base check on 'Gray Dog,' 'Red Rooster,' 'Fox' and 'Codicil of William Arthur Scott.' He was stunned when the word search results had prompted Interpol to call in the United States Secret Service's Economic Stability Division.

He was informed that the Red Rooster was an elderly CIA agent who had retired and been off the international radar for over a year and a half after he had infiltrated a counterfeiting ring in China. Initially, it was thought that the Red Rooster's health had been poor and that he had returned to the States without verifiable results.

However, when Robert Rivers had forwarded the entire Scott codicil to his contacts, after they had already received the initial key words from Harry's sleep-talking, it seemed entirely possible to Interpol that the eccentric CIA agent, William Scott, may have managed to sabotage the counterfeiting operation known as the Fox and Hounds Society after all.

Since there had been no reliable information for

quite some time about this rogue organization, the Red Rooster probably had managed to get hold of their hologram and embedding devices, along with their special inks and one-of-a-kind paper they had developed. Somehow, he got everything out of China and had temporarily shut the Society down.

If this scenario had actually happened, the Scott Codicil was the key to finding the stolen equipment.

They were sorry to learn of Scott's death and hoped that the Rooster's nephew, the FBI agent known as 'Gray Dog,' might be able to assist them in deciphering the messages that his Uncle William had left behind.

Interpol and U.S. Secret Service agents were off to Wisconsin in their surveillance-equipped plane two hours after Robert Rivers had contacted them. It was imperative that they arrive on the scene before any of the fanatical Fox and Hounds Club members. If they did not, and the Club retrieved their stolen equipment, they would be back in China, circulating counterfeit British pounds all over the world within weeks. They had very likely been ready to create their 'perfect pounds' when the Rooster had struck.

Worst case scenario if the Society got their hands on the stash, was that the entire economic stability of the UK might be compromised for years to come. It would have a cataclysmic domino effect as well—not only would the UK face economic ruin, but much of Western Europe would be blindsided and damage control might have to go on for years.

Very little was said driving the four blocks to the Rivers' house from the Scotts' residence. Liffey and Susan sat motionless, staring out of their respective windows, while Harry Scott continued to drift in and out of a troubled sleep.

Finally, Maeve broke the silence and said, "First, we will be parking in our garage, Susan, and then taking your father down by elevator to the safe place. I have already turned the heat on with a remote, and as soon as we get Harry situated, I will come back up to help carry the things you brought and we will all try to settle in as best we can."

"Your mom has been told what's going on and will be picked up at the hospital by a detective from Saint Louis who works for us. They should be here in a few hours, so try to hold on and be brave. You and your parents will be safe with us."

"Safe from *what*, Mrs. Rivers? Why can't you just tell me exactly *what* is going on? I am totally freaking out! No. Strike that. I am *totally terrified*."

"I'm afraid I can't tell you very much, Susan," Maeve Rivers answered, as she drove into the Rivers' three-car garage and closed the door behind them. "Only that it seems your uncle's codicil is about much more than just a hunt for a gold mine. You and Liffey can get back to work on the puzzle as soon as we settle in and I will join you. But now, we need to get down to the safe place."

She lowered Harry Scott on his gurney, using the van lift and walked quickly over to the far-left side of the garage. "I'm going to make sure the elevator is working properly and turn on the lights below. I'll be right back up."

Liffey and Susan stood next to the still sleeping Harry, gaping while they watched Maeve Rivers begin her descent, sinking down under the cement floor like this was all very ordinary.

"I swear I am going to have a heart attack if this kind of spy movie stuff keeps on happening, Liffey!"

"I knew this safe place existed but I was never allowed to see where it was located in case I flapped my big mouth about it by mistake," Liffey said.

Susan began biting her nails. "I am absolutely positive that I'm in one of those nightmares where you know that you are dreaming but you just can't wake up no matter how hard you try."

When Maeve rose up again from below like a magician's assistant, Susan and Liffey pushed Harry Scott over to the elevator platform and began the trip down under.

Liffey was excited. She was about to finally see what her parents had designed and built—a place to be safe if their worst fears were ever realized: that the conflict diamonds trafficker she and her mother had both clashed with, had not died in Alaska after all. That he had somehow survived a polar bear mauling and being tossed into the Arctic Ocean like a bag of potatoes. His body had not turned up and Interpol had their doubts now about his demise.

After what Liffey had witnessed first-hand in Alaska, she had assumed that this man was finally gone forever. Now she was not so sure. Why else would there be this 'safe place' if Interpol did not suspect that the 'Skunk Man' might still be alive?

Nothing could have prepared Liffey and Susan for what they discovered beneath the floor of the garage. Liffey had been told it was a panic or safe 'place,' not a panic or safe 'house' which included four small but colorfully decorated bedrooms, family room with two oversized forest green couches, two beige reclining chairs and a long coffee table stacked with books and magazines.

The glass octagon dining room table, tucked into an alcove off the family room, had soft lighting and an entire wall mural of white cumulus clouds floating above white capped waves crashing on a rocky beach.

There were sea-blue rugs, a computer terminal cubicle, three laptops, a flat screen TV and one full bathroom with tub, shower, a supply of shampoos, conditioners, tissue paper, hand soaps, lotions, tooth brushes with assorted pastes and hair dryer.

Liffey explored the fully-stocked pantry shelves in the kitchen and looked in its huge freezer which contained stacks of pizzas, organic vegetables, frozen yogurt, poultry, beef, fish, fifty packets of wheat bread dough and mozzarella cheeses as big as Max.

"OMG! Mother, where is Max?"

"He's up in the house, Liffey. When Louise gets here, she will bring him up and down regularly. She'll be staying upstairs."

"So then, Max will be able to do his 'you know what' outside in his regular place behind the bushes?"

Maeve masked her exasperation. How could her daughter be thinking of where Max would 'do his you know what business' in the midst of this unexpected crisis?

Liffey turned her attention back to Susan, who looked like the classic definition of 'coming unglued.'

"Actually, if you think about it, this is like the ultimate sleepover pajama party! We will pretend we are eleven years old again and make pancakes and eat pizza and watch movies all day," Liffey suggested.

Susan managed a feeble laugh. "Let's get my poor dad settled into his room, Liffey. Then we can plan our new social life."

"Looking at the bright side here, we're not going to have to study for Miss Minowski's algebra quiz tomorrow now that we are hiding out in our luxury safe house," Liffey pointed out.

"True," Susan agreed, "She would never be able to track us down here!"

"Mr. Simons might be able to find us though," Liffey said. "He's always talking about how much he loves tracking black bears and gathering up their scat."

"What kind of person thinks petrified scat is cool?" Susan said, trying not to dwell on this subject.

"Do you remember that totally disgusting chart he hauled out during Biology?" Liffey groaned.

"Who could ever forget that lecture? Did you know that it can take grasses seven hours to pass through a Black Bear?" Susan finally laughed.

"Duh!" Liffey answered. "Everyone who lives in Wisconsin knows that."

"Does your dad always sleep this much?" Liffey asked, abruptly changing the subject.

"I was just thinking about that," Susan replied, "and the answer is, no, he does not. He slept a lot the first two days after his surgery, but up until today, he had been making good progress, sleeping through the night and only taking one or two short naps during the day."

"Do you think that your Uncle Tom might have slipped something into his pill water while he rifled through your mom's desk?" Liffey continued.

"He might have. Sure. But why would he want my poor father drugged?"

Liffey gave her friend an open palms up, 'you-tell-me' gesture, prompting Susan to answer her own question.

"Oh…I get it. Of course. So he could search our house from top-to-bottom."

CHAPTER SIXTEEN
Pending Arrivals

Jean Rivers was not going to be deterred by white goo. She thought about the early pioneers making their way west, crossing vast plains and valleys in unimaginable weather, looking for a small piece of land they could claim for themselves.

She could almost see herself in a covered wagon, driving fearlessly over bumpy trails and fast flowing streams, not caring in the least what her hair looked like or how rough her soft, white hands had become, or how her fingernails would have been natural and unpainted—possibly even uneven.

Returning to the present, more determined than ever to get to Mineral Point in spite of the snow and flooding concerns, she decided that if her movers would not do the job because of a bit of snow, she would find ones that could.

She was set to make the move first thing in the morning. She could not wait to see the looks on her brother Robert's and everyone else's faces when she casually dropped in, unannounced, to give them the marvelous news that she was now their almost-next-door-neighbor!

John Bergman in New Hampshire was set to go.

Liffey's aunt had changed his reservation and had managed to get him into Madison on a red-eye flight arriving at 7:00 a.m. He hoped that Liffey would be pleasantly surprised and not put out by his visit. His mother had told him several times that "young ladies do not like it when young men turn up unannounced, without an invitation."

Except for one short burst of small hail, Louise's drive to Mineral Point from Illinois was uneventful. The temperature had climbed dramatically and the snow was melting rapidly.

When she reached Dodgeville to transport Ann Scott, there were many angry questions. Mrs. Scott demanded to know why her husband and daughter had been forcibly relocated while she was absent and threatened to call the police. Louise told her the few facts she could reveal—that there was more to the codicil than a treasure hunt for a gold mine and that there were international implications.

For appearances sake, Ann concealed the fact that this news did not particularly surprise her. Her husband, Harry, had never told her much about his supposed 'desk job' with a branch of the FBI in Madison.

Lately, because of illness, he had been on sick leave. Years before he became ill, however, he often had to go off to 'conferences' for weeks at a time, always in places he was not permitted to disclose. It had never sounded much like a desk job to Ann.

Harry's Uncle William had also been some sort of secret agent. She had never been quite sure which intelligence agency William had worked for. He had always been very secretive.

Once, William had completely disappeared from sight for over three years and when he came back to the Point to retire, Harry had instructed her not to ask his uncle any questions—like she was supposed to act as if a three year, unexplained absence from his family, with no word from him, was a normal occurrence?

Like she was not supposed to be even the least bit curious? Like she had not even noticed he had been gone?

When Louise drove into Mineral Point, it was after 10:00 p.m. They were driving by the Scott house when Ann shouted out, "Stop! Tom Scott's truck is parked in our driveway and our garage door is open! What does he think he's doing breaking in like that?"

"Who is he?" Louise asked.

"The brother-in-law from hell," Ann answered.

Louise quickly walked into the open garage and entered the house through the unlocked door.

At first glance, moving from room to room, she saw no one and nothing seemed to be out of order.

It was eerily quiet. No humming refrigerator. No furnace fan.

Had he heard her come in and was just waiting now to make his move?

After a careful, thorough inspection, Louise was

convinced that there was nobody in the house. She gestured outside for Ann Scott to join her to make sure she had not missed any closets or crawl spaces.

After another house walk-through, Ann agreed that Tom Scott was not in there.

"So why is his truck parked out in our driveway," Ann asked, "and the garage door unlocked?"

"He might have run out the back door when he heard me looking around, even though I made very little noise," Louise said.

When Louise filled Ann in about her brother-in-law's alarming behavior towards Liffey Rivers on High Street earlier in the day, Ann was horrified.

If Harry were not living in such a fog, none of this would be happening, she thought bitterly.

CHAPTER SEVENTEEN
Puzzles

After Ann Scott had taken her husband's blood pressure, looked into the whites of his eyes and tested his reflexes, she determined that, even if he had been overly medicated by his older brother, he was stable now. She would wake him up in a few hours for a late dinner.

She was delighted to find that this safe house, where she had dreaded coming, seemed more like checking into a nice, if very small, hotel.

"Before we fix dinner, I want to show you the two hidden stairways out of this place," Maeve said, beckoning her guests to follow her into the kitchen.

"Louise, I believe you have already received the house blueprint from Robert?" Louise nodded.

"As all of you would know, we cannot rely on electricity alone, or even the emergency generator system we have installed. In the event that we would have to leave this place, and the lift to the garage is not working, there are alternative ways out."

"There's a hidden stairway behind the kitchen sink," Maeve began as she moved into the small, but well equipped kitchen. "You pull the sink out and away from the wall and the stairs behind it lead directly up and into our dining room. It's like in a movie when someone discovers a hidden door panel when they accidentally lean on a wall. I'll show you."

Maeve handily moved the sink away from the wall. "It only weighs twenty-five pounds. The secret door is behind this Max Fernekes print." She took the valuable lithograph down from the wall, placed it on the sink and pointed out a small knob that had been hidden behind the artwork. "The door is locked so you must first turn this tiny green knob counter-clockwise to release it."

After Maeve turned the three inch knob, the wall moved to the right, revealing a spiral staircase.

"Pinch me, Liffey," Susan said mechanically, as the group moved up the stairs.

On the landing at the top of the staircase, Maeve pointed out the skylight built into the roof and a small knob like the one in the kitchen, attached to an oak paneled wall. She turned it counter-clockwise and pushed the panel open, revealing the Rivers' formal dining room.

"If it's dark outside, a flashlight is right here," Maeve said, pointing to a small table on the landing.

She closed the dining room panel using the same little knob. "From inside the dining room, you only have to push on the lightest panel of wood and it opens automatically."

The dazed group proceeded down the spiral staircase, back into the kitchen. Maeve continued her emergency exits tour, leading her guests into a large bathroom off the main hallway.

"There's another exit I'm going to show you now that will take you out of this house completely and all the way over to the garden shed in our back yard."

"First, you must walk through a fifty-foot long tunnel before you reach the stairs leading up into the shed. The tunnel should be automatically lit up by overhead sensory lights, but if they're off, there is an emergency flashlight on a small table to the right as you enter the tunnel."

"This tub pulls away from the wall just like the kitchen sink does," she said, effortlessly pulling the tub away from the wall and pointing out a small ring on the wall that looked like a washcloth holder. "Just pull this ring towards you and push inward and the hidden door opens. At the other end, there's a knob just like the one in the kitchen that you turn counter-clockwise to get into the shed."

Maeve surveyed her audience and said, "We will not walk through the tunnel and over to the shed now because I think you are all a bit overwhelmed. I know I was when we designed this place!"

After she had closed the secret door and pushed

the bathtub back into position, she led the group a short distance down the hall and announced: "Finally, there is the panic room."

"Like in that movie *Panic Room?*" Susan Scott's demeanor changed from 'this is all very interesting,' to one of extreme alarm. "Aren't we already *in* the panic room?"

Liffey was not particularly surprised to learn that there was yet another hidden room because she knew her father always prepared for the worst scenario, no matter what. Her mother called him, "a professional worry wort." It made perfect sense to Liffey that her dad would probably have had a wonderful time designing this 'end of the world' habitat.

"The panic room is located right underneath the hall," Maeve explained.

"Really? There is yet another room underneath us?" Ann Scott asked wearily.

"You can get to it from both directions if need be. I'll show you." Maeve replied.

Maeve stopped several feet to the left of the bathroom door. On the wall, where a photo of baby Liffey hung from a small hook, she pulled the little hook towards her without removing the picture. This activated a floor spring which popped open a trap door a few inches in the center of the hall.

"It's manually operated." Maeve demonstrated, pulling the door up and open.

"If our power is cut off and we need to hide immediately, and in the event that we cannot safely use the stairwell exits, we go down here. It's a split-level floor design that was popular in the 1960's."

Ten wide steps with steel banisters on each side led down into a red-carpeted, narrow, short hallway. At the end of the hallway there was a huge steel door that reminded Liffey of an old bank vault she had seen once.

It was unlocked and spring-operated like the trap door. Maeve pulled it open effortlessly in spite of its thickness and obvious weight. "It locks automatically only from the inside," Maeve said, pointing out three dead-bolts on back of the door.

The panic room, like the safe house above them, was tastefully decorated and cozy, approximately half the size of the overhead living quarters.

"Pardon me for asking this Maeve, but why in the world does your family need all this protection? Are you mafia or something?"

Up until this point, Ann Scott, had maintained the non-judgmental mindset of a professional nurse. Now, she pushed her bleached blonde hair bangs away from her flashing dark eyes and focused on Maeve, like a snake ready to lunge and bite.

Susan cringed and turned beet red.

"Mother!" she shouted, "how can you even *think* of something like that, let alone say it out loud?"

Maeve remained unruffled and answered calmly. "No, the Rivers family is not and has never been mafia, Ann. Unfortunately, Liffey and I are at risk because both of us can identify a conflict diamond

119

smuggler. We had reason to believe that he was no longer alive but now intelligence sources cannot guarantee it. So my husband has built this safe house to protect us. Just in case."

"Ironically, we are only here together right now because *your* family is in grave danger. Susan sent Liffey an e-mail last night about meeting up for lunch today and used terms and words which triggered this unfortunate situation."

"Firewalls protected Liffey as the recipient but apparently you have inadequate protection since both Susan's and Liffey's e-mails led to your identity."

Ann Scott looked floored.

"But back to last night," Maeve went on, "when the words and phrases 'gray dog,' 'red rooster,' 'last will and testament,' 'uncle william scott' 'fox,' and 'codicil' were detected in the same e-mail, someone traced it to your home computer's IP and then it was relatively easy finding your street address. You were hacked. I brought your computer here in case your brother-in-law was planning to steal it from the house. Not that it matters anymore."

"Finally, I had my husband run some of those words with Interpol's cyber spying systems and he was told that all of us were now in imminent danger and to get into the safe house immediately."

"We are happy to help you out here but please, do not insult us."

Ann Scott turned beet red like her daughter and said, "I don't know what to say, Maeve. I am very,

very sorry. My nerves have gone down the drain lately and I am clearly not thinking rationally. So then, *we* are the ones who have dragged your family into this mess?"

"Excuse me," Susan said, "I think I am going to go upstairs now and throw up!"

Liffey groaned and ran up the panic room's stairs after her friend.

Maeve cracked a strained smile and said, "Susan could have thrown up down here, there's a bathroom just off the sitting room."

After the tense situation had stabilized, Liffey and Susan sat at the dining room table working where they had left off earlier in the day at the Red Rooster.

Liffey could tell that Susan's mother, who was helping Maeve Rivers prepare dinner, thought they were playing spy or some other kind of children's game when she smiled at them patronizingly—the way lots of adults did when they interacted with their children.

"Okay, Susan. I'm going to get you up to Liffey speed!"

Maeve Rivers smiled and Ann Scott rolled her eyes but also smiled. "Remember how we started talking about the codicil after I told you what your Uncle Tom did to me today on High Street? But then we were interrupted when he showed up at your house again and my mom took him out?"

Maeve looked up from the counter where she

was sitting on a stool waiting for frozen spinach to defrost in the microwave. "Liffey, honey, I don't think you should phrase it quite like that! I did not 'take him out,' I pepper-sprayed him."

"That's what I just said, mother. You took him out!"

Susan giggled and said, "I have to agree with Liffey, Mrs. Rivers, you totally took him out! It was awesome."

"Thank you, Maeve," Ann Scott said. "I don't even want to think about what might have happened if that maniac had managed to break the door down and get his hands on the girls."

"Anyway," Liffey said, "before my mother and I came over to your house, I worked on the puzzle at home for an hour or so while she talked to my dad in South Africa. So, here goes...."

All eyes turned towards Liffey.

"First, it was easy to find an online Chinese-to-English translation service and it only took a few seconds for it to translate the Chinese characters above the crowing rooster cartoon into English. The translation said:

MEATLOAF TO GO
OR EAT HERE EVERYDAY

It's almost the exact same message that's on the Red Rooster's sign which is:

PASTY DAILY TO GO OR EAT HERE."

Liffey could tell from the blank expressions on everyone's faces that they were not following her translation trend of thought.

"I think that the most confusing thing here is which one of these messages did Uncle William want us to unscramble? Which one of them is the possible anagram—the Chinese translation into English words or the English words already on the Rooster's sign?"

Ann interrupted. "Unscramble? What do you mean?"

"I'm pretty sure that the Rooster's sign is an anagram, Mrs. Scott, and I'm good at them! You know, an anagram, like when you re-arrange all the letters in a sentence or a phrase and then it says something else."

"Some easy examples of scrambled up words that are animal anagrams would be:

act = cat
god=dog

Before I found my mother, my dad and I used to solve anagrams every night from the puzzle pages in the newspapers he subscribed to. We used Scrabble letters to make it easier."

"So, I guess what I'm doing now is bragging about how good I am at doing puzzles. And I'm fast. My dad used to time us and the one with the best time at the end of each week got to pick where we ate out for dinner on Sundays."

"Since I would basically kill for shrimp fried rice and my dad was totally sick of Chinese food, we had a real competitive thing going on for a long time."

Susan jumped in: "OMG! You've figured it out

already Liffey? I knew you would help but not so quickly!"

"No, no! Slow down Susan! I have not figured it all out!"

"What *did* you come up with then, Liffey?" Ann Scott inquired. This time she did not have the smug, patronizing look on her face.

"I found Scrabble letters for the all the words on the Rooster sign and fooled around with them and the meatloaf Chinese translation too."

"There were some common words and phrases in both the English and Chinese versions, like 'Go Or Eat Here.' But the word meatloaf in the Chinese translation did not lead me to any kind of scrambled up message, so then I concentrated only on the Red Rooster sign's words in English to see if they might work and here's what I came up with:

PASTY DAILY TO GO OR EAT HERE
could be an anagram for:
RARE PAYLOAD SITE GO TO THE Y."

The expressions on Ann, Susan and Maeve's faces tried to mask their shared disappointment.

"That's it?" asked Susan, visibly let down.

"So far, yes." Liffey frowned. "Remember, I only fooled around with it for an hour or so."

"Well, what does it *mean*?" Susan demanded.

"You tell me Susan!" Liffey was beginning to get annoyed with the negative vibes coming at her from all directions.

"I found one more thing that might make sense to someone," Liffey said.

"There is a picture of a tea cup and a spoon that might be a rebus puzzle."

No one said a word.

The Scotts looked confused.

"You know, a rebus puzzle. It's a puzzle made up of images or words and usually a combination of both which represent a word or a phrase."

Maeve cut in when it was obvious that the Scotts were not getting it.

"An easy example of a rebus puzzle would be the phrase, TOP SECRET with the word SECRET written several times, one on top of the other with an arrow pointing at the *top* SECRET in the stack. The answer would be 'Top Secret.' I'll show you."

Maeve wrote: **>SECRET<**
               SECRET
               SECRET

and drew two arrows pointing at the first SECRET on top of the stack. The Scotts' faces lit up when they got it.

Liffey started up again. "That's a great example. Sooo…I think the rebus puzzle in the codicil is the picture of the tea cup with the spoon and maybe it means 'stir coffee' or 'coffee spoon' or 'stir tea' or…"

Susan suddenly began to scream hysterically, like she had gone out of control at a boy band concert.

"Susan Scott!" her mother said, "for heaven's sake,

calm down! What on earth is wrong with you?"

"You actually *know* what 'Stir-Tea' means, don't you Susan?" Liffey asked.

"I had a feeling that your Uncle William might give you a clue that no one else would be able to figure out so the gold mine would go to your family."

The excited glow suddenly drained from Susan's face and she turned pale, like she might faint.

Liffey took control and said, "All right then. We need you to breathe slowly now, Susan. Try to calm down and tell us what you are remembering and Mother, please take notes."

Maeve nodded, barely able to contain her own excitement at this amazing breakthrough.

"Tell us, what does 'Stir-Tea' mean to you, Susan, and take your time," Liffey said.

Susan drew in a few extra gulps of oxygen and began her trip down memory lane.

"Uncle William used to take me out exploring in the country when he would come back to town after being gone for a long time. We used to go to a place that he called 'the secret ridge.'"

"I remember, Susan," Ann Scott said softly. "You always came home after those outings like you had discovered the secrets of the universe."

"Anyway," Susan pressed on, "he called our little expeditions, 'exploration maneuvers,' and I took it all very seriously."

"I was probably about six-years-old when we did most of the secret ridge exploring. Uncle William was always gone by the time I was seven and sometimes a few years would pass before I would see him again."

"I can remember that at the bottom of a small hill, there was a limestone ridge that was only about three feet wide and two feet high, but it was very long. It seemed as long as a football field."

"I used to walk along that ridge, very unsteadily, holding a green willow branch from the big tree in his front yard. I remember it was always shaped like a Y. It had to be shaped like a Y."

"Oh my goodness," Ann murmured, "it's the Y from Liffey's anagram."

Susan did not comment on her mother's remark and continued her story.

"Like I said, the branch, or big twig, always had to be shaped like a Y—he called it a 'dousing' stick. I remember because he said it was like getting doused with water. He said if the stick started acting crazy, it meant we were near gold or some kind of mineral deposit that was not too far down in the rock."

"I told you once Liffey, how the glaciers missed this area? Well, because those glaciers missed us, it means that mineral deposits are close to the surface and fairly easy to get at."

"That's why so many miners were able to make money around this area, they only needed picks to get at the lead deposits."

"So, anyway, I would walk along the long rock formation holding the Y stick in front of me, upside down, and he would say: 'Sturdy as you go now,

127

Susan. Sturdy.' I would always reply very indignantly, 'I *am* **STIR-TEA**, Uncle William.' Then he would laugh and laugh."

"One time, a Y stick went crazy and was pulling down so hard that it felt like I had a big fish tugging on a pole. I think I started to cry because it scraped my hands."

"Uncle William said something like, he was very sorry about my scraped hands, but that I had just discovered something and it might be gold."

"He said we would have to get ourselves some mining equipment and then come back to remove whatever it was out from the limestone ridge."

"Liffey, this entire codicil was meant for me to figure out but I never could have done it without you! I had completely forgotten about using Y sticks and looking for mineral deposits along that ridge with Uncle William because after that day, we never got around to actually digging for anything."

"At least *I* never dug for it with him. I guess he must have done some digging alone though," Susan thought out loud. "Actually, I don't remember ever going back there again with Uncle William after that day."

"None of the Scotts would have ever figured it out, Liffey. I know I certainly wouldn't have," Ann Scott admitted.

"I still remember how to get to that secret ridge too," Susan said, gathering steam.

"It's right next to that big red barn southwest of

town on County Road O that says, **New Baltimore 1838**, on the side of it. I'm absolutely sure I can find the ridge easily again because it's so long."

"We can go for a look as soon as the snow melts. The weather channel says it's going to be in the high forties tomorrow," Susan said hopefully. "It will be muddy and gross but that's why boots were invented, right?"

"You know, I think William did own some land over near that barn," Ann Scott said. "I had forgotten all about it. Attorney Sarah Wood is going to probate his estate. She said there is a mountain of paperwork to sort through. But the codicil made it clear that whoever finds the gold will own it. And that person will be you, Susan!"

A voice sounded from the hallway: "Susan, we're not going anywhere until this is all over," Harry Scott said, moving into the living room area.

"Pops, I'm so glad you're finally awake! Liffey and I have figured out the location of the gold mine!"

"That's wonderful, Susan, but I meant what I said about not going anywhere until we are told we are safe."

"Oh, that's right, you slept through most of it! We're safe from Uncle Tom now, Pops. Mrs. Rivers pepper-sprayed him when he tried to kick in my bedroom door and he was escorted out of the house when the police arrived. We just hope they put him in jail."

Harry slowly sat down in the closest recliner chair

and said, "How I wish that your Uncle Tom was all we had to worry about now, Susan."

"He's like a tiny grain of sand on a mile-long beach," Harry said dramatically.

"I was so excited about the gold mine, I forgot to think about why we are really down here hiding underground!" Susan said.

"I guess it's because I sent that e-mail to Liffey last night and now some evil empire is coming after all of us? I honestly just don't get it, Pops."

"I am guessing there's probably a lot more going on here than locating a gold mine too," Liffey agreed.

"I'll start from the beginning," Harry announced.

"I will be telling this story a hundred times when the Feds get here, so I may as well rehearse it some," Harry said resignedly, "and a million thanks to Maeve Rivers for alerting her husband about my strange outburst."

"It is remarkable that she suspected the serious nature of my sleep-talk ranting."

"You probably saved my life, Maeve, and possibly the financial stability of Western Europe. Writing up that outline of what has happened so far and leaving it for me on my bedside table was very thoughtful, even though it confirmed my worst fears."

Harry Scott's eyelids fluttered and he drifted off for a few seconds but then took a sip of water and rallied.

"Once upon a time," he began again, "there was a Gray Dog and a Red Rooster who went off into the world seeking adventure…"

He coughed and began to snore peacefully.

His obviously frustrated wife, tucked him in with a throw-blanket over his afghan and pulled the foot rest up.

"I mean really. The financial stability of Western Europe?" Maeve muttered as she walked towards her bedroom. "Robert really needs to get here and fill all of us in on this 'plot,' or whatever it is that's going on."

Ann Scott trailed behind, exasperated.

Susan was hiccupping loudly on her way to the bedroom she was sharing with Liffey.

"Are you coming, Liffey?" she managed to get out between spasms.

"Soon," Liffey replied. "First, I'm going to try to figure out what I missed in your uncle's codicil about Western Europe's entire economy collapsing while I practice my Slip Jig for the feis next weekend."

"Sure. That's a great idea Liffey. You go figure out how the entire economy of Europe is going to collapse while you practice your Slip Jig. We sound like patients in a mental hospital."

Liffey was inclined to agree with her friend but she had discovered over the years that practicing her Irish dance steps while she pondered things that were bothering her, often gave her mental clarity and this codicil puzzle was becoming overwhelming.

"What's a Slip Jig anyway?" Susan called halfway down the hall over her shoulder.

"Actually, never mind. I don't think I need any more useless information filed in my head tonight."

"I'm going to bed now, Liffey. See you tomorrow morning. That is, of course, if the world doesn't end by then. Or whatever...." Susan's voice trailed off.

This has become sooo much more exciting than finding a gold mine. Who can sleep?

CHAPTER EIGHTEEN
Betrayal

Louise Anderson pushed fifteen small levers down to their 'off' positions and pressed ten small buttons, effectively shutting down all of the multi-layered security systems Robert Rivers had installed.

She attached listening devices to the phone lines so that all incoming and outgoing calls would now be monitored and recorded.

I guess I've made up my mind which side I'm on, she thought uneasily, not at all certain that she had made the right decision. She wished no harm to come to the Rivers family and there would be no harm with her here running things.

All she needed to do was to collect information as to the location of a hidden gold mine which also contained—? Louise was miffed that her anonymous employer had used a phone voice modifier to conceal his real voice, and had also declined to reveal what he was really looking for, only hinting that there was far more at stake than a hidden gold deposit.

"So much for safe houses," she said to herself. She would plant more sophisticated surveillance bugs downstairs at dawn tomorrow and begin to monitor conversations until she picked up on the location of whatever it was that someone was willing to pay her a fortune to help find.

Liffey quickly discovered that there was not enough space in the kitchen to do a proper Slip Jig. Since she did not want to wake up Harry Scott, she decided to sneak upstairs using the hidden stairway behind the kitchen and bring Max back down here with her for the night. They would sleep on the couch.

Liffey was fairly confident that her tiny terrier would not wake up while she was abducting him because he had always been an unreliable watch dog and could sleep through anything.

She moved the kitchen sink out, removed the Fernekes print from the wall, turned the door knob counter clockwise and heard the lock pop open.

Max had better not start barking this late in his career as a useless watch dog, she thought.

There were twenty-two steps. When she arrived at the top of the stairs, she saw the light illuminating the small knob her mother had demonstrated earlier, turned it counter-clockwise and pushed the dining room panel open.

So far, so good. No barking.

Liffey walked quietly through the dining room, down the hallway and into her bedroom where Max was snuggling contentedly with his blankie on her pillow. As Liffey had expected, he was in a deep sleep and did not make a sound. She picked him up gently and started back to the open panel in the dining

134

room.

The guest room door where Louise was sleeping remained closed and she was able to make it through the house undetected.

As the dining room panel closed behind her, she was startled to see that the main surveillance control panel for her father's security monitoring systems was completely dark. Alarms, lights, video cameras and recording devices had all been turned off. It appeared that the shutdown had been deliberate and that there was not some kind of malfunction going on. She had not noticed this on her way up because the control panel was on the wall in back of her when she had entered the dining room.

Liffey rearranged Max in her arms and pulled the levers back up to their 'on' positions, watching as one by one, they started blinking green again.

Only her mother and herself had been up here in the house today.

And Louise.

Louise had deposited the very rattled Ann Scott in the safe house by way of the garage elevator, said a quick "hey," did the house tour and then quickly exited through the garage again. She had presumably let herself into the main house the conventional way, using the front door house key Maeve had handed to her before she left.

Liffey tried very hard to come up with plausible reasons why Louise might have had to shut down all of their surveillance systems and then leave them off.

After her head began thumping, Liffey had to admit that she could not think of any acceptable circumstances under which someone would decide to switch off an entire security system and not bother telling the others—unless that someone actually did not want the premises, or the people on the premises, to be protected.

This frightening, awkward turn of events, would have to be addressed first thing in the morning, as soon as Louise discovered that Max was missing.

Louise stood at the top of the stairwell watching all the lights on the surveillance panel flashing green.

Somehow, Liffey had managed to get in up here last night and had removed Max without waking her. Then, before returning to the safe house below, she had turned all the security systems back on again.

Liffey knew.

CHAPTER NINETEEN
Arrivals

John Bergman arrived in Madison, Wisconsin, on time. When he walked out into the Passenger Arrivals area, he was greatly surprised to see Liffey's Aunt Jean holding a huge sign on a stick that said:

JOHN BERGMAN !
WELCOME !
WISCONSIN LOVES YOU !!!

He felt like he should be some kind of celebrity from Wisconsin being greeted with a sign like that, when the truth was, this was the first time he had ever set foot in the state.

However, having met Jean Rivers on the Alaskan Sun cruise ship last spring, he was well aware that things could be much more embarrassing than this because he had seen her in action. He was fairly certain that there could be no one else on earth as peculiar as Jean Rivers, but he did like her a lot. And she was Liffey's only aunt which gave her immediate status—insane or otherwise.

He had followed Jean's directions not to say anything to her niece about his coming to help Jean with her move to Mineral Point. Now he wished he had not honored this promise. *I am aiding and abetting a lunatic ambush on the Rivers family*, he realized, giving her a welcoming hug.

"John, *darling*! How wonderful to see you! You are even more handsome than I remember! Let's pick up your luggage, dear."

"All I brought is right here on my back, Jean. I'm only going to be here two days."

"You mean you have no luggage with you?" Jean Rivers looked perplexed.

"Just my back pack."

"You have no luggage?"

John was starting to worry about his having no luggage as it was obviously upsetting Jean Rivers.

"I do have clothes in my backpack and personal items."

"But no luggage?"

John was starting to fear that this conversation had no ending, like in "The Song That Never Ends."

"No luggage. Just my backpack."

"I see. No luggage?"

John quickly realized that the concept of having no luggage was totally incomprehensible for Jean and said, "But I *do* have a full set of luggage at home and brought most of those bags along with me on the Alaskan cruise."

This information seemed to greatly comfort Jean. She sighed and said, "I see. We're good to go then, but not to Baggage Claims."

"Right," John replied, trying hard not to sound as impatient as he felt. "We'll just leave the airport now and find your car."

He gritted his teeth, anticipating Jean Rivers' final comment and was prepared for it when it came.

"So then, we won't need a trolley for your bags because you didn't bring any luggage."

He smiled from ear to ear and said, "exactly!"

Robert Rivers munched on a piece of Biltong and sipped decaffeinated green tea as he tried to keep worried thoughts from clouding up his thinking. He needed to sleep on this flight but so far had not been able to even cat nap. Why hadn't Louise gotten back to him yet with a status report? It wasn't like her not to keep him informed at regular intervals. But surely if something had gone terribly wrong, Maeve would have called him? That was peculiar too because he had left three messages for her to call him back with an update.

Louise must have advised everyone to turn their phones off, or perhaps they had lost coverage during the massive snowstorm that had hit the Midwest so hard. He had to stop worrying and get some sleep or he would be useless when he finally arrived back in Wisconsin.

He trusted Maeve to keep things together. But then, why hadn't she called?

Liffey and Max were sound asleep on the living room

couch when Max began to growl quietly under his breath like he did if he thought there was a mouse in the room. He stopped when Liffey put the sock of the week back into his mouth.

Harry Scott was snoring loudly in the reclining chair next to the couch.

Liffey pretended to be asleep while she listened to padded footsteps coming from inside the kitchen. It had to be Louise. Things had certainly changed. Now Max was perceiving her supposed bodyguard and friend to be a threat.

Since there were no windows in the safe house and her phone was in her bedroom, Liffey had no idea what time it was.

She guessed that Louise was only down here now because she was going to plant electronic bugs and then go back upstairs to listen in to their private conversations—after the inevitable conversation they would soon be having about the turned off security systems. Liffey was curious as to what kind of lies Louise would make up to explain her actions.

Liffey still could not think of how to broach this subject tactfully. Tactfulness had never come easily to her under the very best of circumstances.

Liffey sadly realized she could not just ignore the prickling sensations which had started up again at the same time Max had begun to growl. Louise was no longer her friend and protector. She was now her worst enemy.

It would be no use for Liffey to try to mask her

grim discovery with false bravado. Louise must know by now that Liffey had found the disabled security systems and Liffey knew that Louise always carried a handgun. It was emotionally draining for Liffey to think about Louise as her adversary, but the pins and needles had never steered her in the wrong direction. They always signaled imminent danger.

The only way Liffey could see not being totally torpedoed by her predicament, was to somehow get the gun away from Louise and take control of this unfortunate development before the others woke up. According to her mother, when the bedroom doors were closed, the rooms down here were soundproof. So maybe she could confront Louise, take her gun and then lock her up in the hallway closet without creating too much commotion.

Her mother had not actually told her that the hall closet down here could be locked, but Liffey had a hunch that it could be and that her mother had just not mentioned it because it had seemed unimportant.

Liffey was basing this wild thinking on a game she and her dad used to play years ago. He usually won their mental 'what if' challenges as to how to resolve tricky, dangerous situations.

"You must *always*, *always*, *always* have a place where you can lock up someone before calling the police for assistance, Liffey—like say a hall closet. It could save your life."

Liffey was counting on her father's having taken his own advice here because if he had not, she did not have any Plan B and she only had a very 'iffy' Plan A.

Plan A was not much but it was all that Liffey could come up with on thirty seconds notice. She knew that Max the Magnificent was a deep sleeper. If her desperate hunch was right, in his sleepy stupor, it might be possible to give him the attack command she had successfully used against the blue clown member of the Joyful Jesters some months ago when Max had totally come through for her.

The odds had certainly been stacked against a tiny terrier that could fit inside a tote bag, bringing a grownup clown-man down to his knees. But Max had done it brilliantly after Liffey spent a week training him to attack a non-destructible toy clown.

Max suddenly stopped growling and had slipped into what looked like a delta sleep cycle to Liffey. This was not good. A rapid eye movement cycle would be much better for the emergency at hand. She could tell that Max's eyes were not moving under his eyelids.

She needed to remember exactly what she had said to Max in the situation with the menacing clown. It was hard to believe now that she had once turned Max into a ferocious, heel-biting attack weapon. He looked like a little ball of fur.

It seemed too simple, but Liffey recalled that all she had actually said was: "Attack Max," or was it "Max Attack?"

If Max could just relive his attack on the clown's

ankle in this delta wave sleep cycle, the odds would only be about 100 to 1 *against* him successfully taking Louise down.

Not great odds, she realized, but who would have ever thought until yesterday that her petite, mild-mannered mother, could have turned a six-foot, loud-mouthed bully into quivering jello on the floor?

It's going to be entirely up to you, Max, she whispered into his fuzzy little ear, trying to reconstruct exactly what she had programmed Max to do to the clown.

She decided that the sock was too soft to hurl at Louise's ankles. She needed something hard, like the plastic clown toy she had thrown at the blue clown's feet.

The TV remote would have to do.

Max's wheezy breathing was blending in nicely with Harry Scott's common dozing noises, allowing Liffey a bit of noise cover while she looked for the remote. The kitchen night light provided enough illumination for her to see that it was not on the coffee table.

She tried to remain calm and groped under the couch cushion, which was the next logical place to look for a television remote.

It was there.

Liffey could hear Louise quietly opening and closing cupboards in the kitchen. Was she going to block that escape route?

Next, Louise crept around the living room area and briefly went into the computer cubicle. She had to be planting bugs.

Liffey willed herself not to open her eyes for a look-see because she could not risk Louise's picking up on some kind of vibe she might unintentionally transmit.

Max needs to jump at her ankles the second she comes over to see if I'm awake. She must have planted listening devices all over by now, so whoever wants to know what's going on down here will hopefully soon hear Louise screaming when Max makes his move.

Liffey was ready.

CHAPTER TWENTY
The Cemetery

In her loft above the kitchen, Jane hurriedly dressed for school, listening expectantly for breakfast conversation coming from below, but it was silent.

She was very disappointed after she had climbed down the ladder and discovered that her cousins had already left.

Mam told her last night that she was going over to visit Mrs. O'Hare early this morning. A fresh loaf of untouched soda bread, large scoop of creamy butter and a small pot of still-warm tea were on the table. Patrick and Da must have gone out to the hayfields already.

Jane poured some tea and ripped off a piece of bread, wondering why her cousins had left without saying farewell.

She had been looking forward to having more conversation with them over breakfast. After a few gulps of tea, she decided she would eat the soda bread on her way to school.

Mam had placed her school satchel by the front door. Jane could smell the delicious ham from last night's feast packed away in it for her lunch today. Her chalkboard slate, instead of being packed up, rested next to the bag, which was odd. Mam was usually very careful to make sure everything she thought her daughter might need during the day had made it into the satchel.

She picked up the slate and saw that there was something written on it. Up until this moment, Jane had only read notes from Mary Southwick during school when Mr. Heaton's back was turned.

Jane had never seen such beautiful writing used in real life before. Mr. Heaton had demonstrated how to form lovely capital letters like these once and said he would teach his students the Spencerian Script Method of Penmanship when they were a bit more advanced.

Since then, Mr. Heaton's class had only practiced writing printed letters on their slates. Like the ones that were in books.

The only letter on her slate now that she was sure of was a capital 'A.' It had a little slanted line above it. Jane had no idea why. Maybe it was a slip of hand error.

How was she ever going to manage to preserve these exquisite letters in her memory until she could find out what they were? The letters would be erased from both the slate and her head in no time and then be gone forever.

She might never see such elegant writing again. She wondered which of her cousins it was that had

146

learned how to write this way. She would not have figured that either of them would have been able to do this. If only she had a pen and ink and paper, she might be able to copy them and get them translated.

But I can scratch them on to the back of a kitchen chair, she thought. *When Mam gets angry, I will tell her I only did it to commemorate last night.*

Somehow she had to protect this writing until she got to school and Mr. Heaton could tell her what the fancy letters were. Then she could sound them out to make the word.

She knew Da and Mam could read a wee bit but since neither of them had ever been to school, it was unlikely that they would know how to translate these elaborate letters into the word they formed.

After she had carefully etched each letter on to the back of her own chair, she happily remembered that her brother had permission to miss school all day today to help Da bale hay.

She enjoyed walking to school alone, keeping her own company and not being tormented by her older sibling.

Hopefully, most of the other boys in her school would also have chores to do during these weeks before the cold winds from Canada brought early winter snow showers.

It had been nice being at school last year at this time with only Mary Southwick and two other girls who, like herself, actually *wanted* to be there to learn. The boys were mostly interested in showing off and making the girls' lives miserable.

Except for life-threatening, freezing days during winter, when she and Patrick were driven to school by wagon, Jane walked the three miles each way to and from Mineral Point.

Mam had told her once that the weather was never so bitterly cold over in Ireland when she was growing up in County Sligo.

But then, there was no money and never enough food because the landlord got most of her family's crops and sold them in the Dublin markets so he could afford to live in his fine house.

Mam said that her family, the McDermotts, were 'tenants' in Ireland and that meant that they did not really own the little piece of land they farmed.

"If we did not have this farm, Jane, we would be eating poorly like we did in Sligo, when nearly all that we grew, except for some of the potatoes and a few cabbages, went to our landlord," Mam had said.

So apparently the milder weather in Ireland had not benefited her mam's family much and certainly had not given them an easier life, Jane reflected.

Mam had recently said that she was very worried lately because one of the older church fussbudgets had recently heard from home that there were going to be food shortages soon in County Mayo, which was right next to Sligo. Some of the potato crops had failed that year in Mayo. "But next year will make up for it, I'm sure," Mam had said optimistically.

"There will not be potato blights in Sligo again. Lord knows we have already had our share of those catastrophes."

Jane was sorely tempted to ask her mam about the potato blights in Sligo that had happened 'before' but her mam's eyes had gotten all blurry with tears—like she was only saying that because she was not at all certain that more potato problems were going to spare Sligo in the future. Which meant that there had to have already been at least several potato blights *before* in Sligo, but Mam had never mentioned them until now.

Mam recovered from her tears and said, "Here in Wisconsin, sure we nearly freeze to death when we go outside during the late winter months, but we eat well every single day of the entire year and, thanks to my sister, Mary, may she and her husband Robert Jones rest in peace, we Scotts will always own this fertile land we live on."

Jane found herself leaping and twirling all over the road on her way to school that morning. It was easy to hold both of her arms down stiffly by her sides because she put her own slate in her right hand to protect the chalk letters and Patrick's slate tucked inside her satchel bag, weighted down her left arm evenly with her right. The weather today was much cooler following yesterday's heat wave. It made her want to dance like Mam had done last night.

She could not stop thinking about all the fiddling

149

and seeing her mam jumping up and down like that with her feet pounding on the floor boards.

Jane had never seen anything like it before. It had thrilled her and she wanted more of the same.

Just as remarkable as her mam's flying feet, was her da playing that fiddle. Until last night, when his cousin Levi went outside to his saddle bags and brought his own fiddle into the house, Jane had never imagined such a thing ever happening in front of her hearth.

Mam had walked into their kitchen and retrieved a fiddle that was all wrapped up in an old blanket, from underneath the floor boards in the pantry, like it was an ordinary after dinner ritual.

Mam said that it belonged to Da and when Da had begun to play, keeping time with his cousins, and her mam had started leaping around the room, Jane thought that perhaps she had died and gone straight to heaven.

Da had looked pained last night, after he had settled his cousins down in the barn, when she had asked him why Patrick and she had never, in their entire lives, heard him even *once* play his wonderful fiddle or seen their mam dance.

Da shook his head sadly and told her that they were Americans now, not Irish, and the old ways had to be forgotten so that they would fit in better over here.

Jane switched from all the dancing and twirling to walking slowly on the road into town, thinking about 'fitting in' and exactly what that was supposed to mean.

Up until her da had said that, she thought that she already did 'fit in.' Was that only because her parents had shielded her from Irish fiddle music and dancing and other Irish things?

There had always been a cloudy memory in her head of sitting by the sea in Ireland, listening to her parents talking to each other in some kind of foreign language—except that in this shadowy recollection, she had understood what they were talking about!

Did Irish people have their own language? Like the Cornish here in Iowa County did and the Welsh too?

If they did, the Irish did not speak it publicly. Everybody she knew who had come here from Ireland spoke only English in public, no matter how peculiar it might sound.

At church, even the oldest Irish biddies always spoke English and sometimes a little Latin if they wanted to impress someone.

Jane thought about it. She *had* noticed that after Mass on Sundays, most of the biddies whispered amongst one another—like they were telling secrets. She thought it was extremely rude behavior and that they must be gossiping, which was a sin.

She could never make out exactly what they were saying though. Even when she got up close enough to hear clearly and listen in, it always sounded like nonsense. Were they speaking Irish words?

As she passed by Mrs. Gibbons' chicken coops, she thought about how her da worked in the local lead mines each year when their family harvest was over and before Patrick and he started up plowing again in the spring. She knew that there were many Irish men who worked in the mines with him.

Perhaps they spoke Irish to each other down in those mines, twenty feet under the ground, if there really was such a language? She would ask Mam.

Mary Southwick had confessed to her last year that her mother, Sarah Southwick, had cautioned her to "be careful around that Jane Scott girl" and "not to let all those ignorant Irish words and customs rub off on you."

At the time, Jane thought that her friend had been mistaken and that Mary's mother had simply meant that some of the Irish around Mineral Point had strange accents when they spoke English.

Now she was not so sure.

Sometimes at Mass during his preaching, Father Mazzuchelli forgot that he was preaching to English-speaking people and would start using lovely Italian words.

Jane thought that Italian was a beautiful foreign language and wished she knew how to speak it.

Maybe she had spoken a foreign language too before they had moved here to Wisconsin when she was only three?

It was nice having all these deep thoughts while she walked along by herself on her way to school.

Jane had decided to stop by the cemetery before classes started up for the day and had left the house an hour before she needed to this morning, even though the graveyard was only a few blocks from Mr. Heaton's school.

At the cemetery gate, she put Patrick's slate into her school bag, carefully propped up her own slate with its beautiful letters next to it, and reached deep down into her dress pocket for the hambone she had taken without her mam's permission—in case Mr. Caffee's dog was in the vicinity.

She said a quick *Ave* for Mr. Caffee and began walking past many big monuments and grave markers which were permanently saluting the people from Mineral Point who had been well-thought-of.

Way in the back of the untended, farthest end of the graveyard, there were a few crudely fashioned wooden crosses peeking up over tall prairie grasses and a jungle of tangled, overgrown weeds.

Jane made up her mind to come here early next spring, after the last snow, and scatter the thousands of wildflower seeds she had collected and saved in a jar over the years. Now she knew why she had been saving them.

Back in the weedy section of the cemetery, Mr. Caffee and the others who rested there with him, would be able to enjoy their own colorful, private garden late next spring and all the way up to the snowfall next year in late autumn. Some of the souls back there with her cousin were only there because their families did not have the means to bury them, let alone to put up a gravestone. Mam said that back in Ireland, tenants' graves were usually marked with some sort of smallish rock taken from a field.

Jane knew that Mary Southwick and many others would harshly judge her for planting flowers next to a murderer's grave, but she would let the Good Lord sort all of that out and follow her heart.

Maybe the flowers would comfort some of the families belonging to the small wooden crosses too. Mam had told her once that many Catholics could not be buried in their own church graveyards because they had committed mortal sins that made them unfit to be buried in consecrated ground.

Father Mazzuchelli had preached several times that all sins could be forgiven—even at the very moment of death, if the sinner was very sorry for having committed them. If the sinner forgot to repent, he said he was sure that God would have a way of revealing to this sinner the damage and pain caused by the sins he or she had committed. Father said that every so often he could hear the sorrowful sighs of sinners in their afterlife.

On top of a lonely heap of fresh black dirt, far back by the cemetery's wooden fence boundary, a gray dog methodically gnawed on a large beef bone.

CHAPTER TWENTY-ONE
Max Attack

John Bergman had not been this carsick since he was five. He wished now that he had not scarfed down that breakfast burrito at the Madison airport before they had set off for Mineral Point.

Why did this lady ride the brakes like that?

No wonder Liffey had stopped going to her Irish dancing classes in Milwaukee until her mother was home again.

She had told him it was pointless because driving with her Aunt Jean, especially over long distances, always made her feel desperately ill.

Now he knew what Liffey had been talking about. He hoped Mineral Point was not too much farther. He figured he had another twenty minutes maximum before he would have to ask Jean Rivers to pull over to the side of the road where he would leave his breakfast behind in a ditch.

Liffey concentrated on the floor next to her by the couch, resisting a strong impulse to sit up and scan her surroundings. She gripped the remote tightly, ready to hurl it at Louise's feet when she got close enough.

Max was normally a contented, passive dog. He growled only if he saw a mouse, because he knew it was safe for him to intimidate creatures that could squeeze through small holes.

Liffey could only hope and pray that he had stored the memory of his encounter with the clown's ankle somewhere in his small brain.

What Liffey was not at all sure about was what she needed to do after Max did his part, if he *did* do his part, and chomped down on Louise's ankle.

Should she jump on Louise and try to tackle her? What if Louise already had her handgun out?

Or, should she too go for Louise's ankles like Max would hopefully do?

I guess I'll just have to see what happens, she thought, trying not to think about all the awful outcomes that were likely for this lame plan.

For one thing, she had no idea whatsoever how she was going to lock Louise in the hall closet or whether or not it even could be locked.

Another daunting thing to think about was that Louise was way bigger that she was and trained in martial arts and who knew what else?

Liffey had been a casualty once before in a girl fight back in her old black-hole-middle-school when she had been body slammed against a hallway wall.

She shuddered now, remembering how much that had hurt. All she had been trying to do was to get past the girls to her locker.

How did she think she was now going to be able to get six-foot-tall Louise into that hall closet all by herself? Maybe this was a really, really bad idea after all...

When Liffey heard the sink being pushed back again against the wall in the kitchen, she tensed. The inevitable showdown with Louise was about to take place.

Or maybe not.

She still did not know exactly what she was going to do.

She could only hope that Louise would not think that she was stupid enough to actually try what she *was actually* going to try and would come over to the couch empty-handed.

Max stirred in Liffey's arms and she could feel a low vibration rising up from his stomach as Louise approached.

She fervently hoped he was not dreaming about a mouse.

Timing was everything.

If I mess up the toss, it's all over.

"Liffey, wake up, it's Louise. I think we need to talk."

Liffey had still not quite decided what to do. She figured she had at least another five seconds to make up her mind.

"Liffey, you *need* to wake up now," Louise hissed in a low, threatening voice that Liffey had never heard her use before.

That tone did it!

Liffey tossed the TV remote hard at Louise's feet and yelled: **"MAX ATTACK!"**

Like in a dream, Max responded even better than she had dared hope. He was like a Ninja warrior, using the element of surprise to his advantage.

He dove right off the couch without hesitation and landed on Louise's feet where he immediately began to chew on her right ankle like the lethal ankle weapon Liffey had trained him to be.

Even though she was well aware that his tiny dog teeth would probably hurt less than a teething human baby's bite, Liffey knew that it was the unexpected shock, like getting dunked in a swimming pool from behind, or a neighbor's pet dog jumping up on you unexpectedly, that threw someone off balance.

Before Louise could let out a loud protest, Liffey jumped up and tackled her at the knees.

Not expecting such an effective offensive move, Louise went down hard and Liffey immediately jumped on her chest, frantically trying to figure out what she should to do next before Louise would probably send her flying across the room.

Before it came to that, a voice sounded in the

semi-darkness.

"It's okay now Liffey, I've got your back. Stand up slowly and then walk backwards towards me. Keep your eyes fixed on the lady on the floor."

The voice belonged to Harry Scott.

"You on the floor! Roll over on to your stomach and put your hands above your head."

"Where do professionals hide their guns these days?" Harry Scott asked, like he was used to this kind of situation.

"I am thinking it would probably be strapped to your shoulder or side and that makes it difficult to trust you to take it out and toss it to the side of you. So this is what I'm going to do…"

Harry bent down and what happened next was like a flash of bright lightning—Liffey saw the action unfold but could not quite process it.

Louise rolled over twice, grabbing her gun from its holster during the second roll over. But before she could point it at someone, Harry Scott aimed his pen at her and she went limp.

Liffey was flabbergasted.

Had she just seen Mr. Scott shoot something out of a *pen* that had knocked Louise unconscious?

"I really hate it when I have to do that to people," Harry said sincerely.

"It seems to come with the territory these days."

"I normally prefer being out in the field with plain old pepper spray. These mini tranquilizing darts are very unpredictable."

159

"Sometimes, and usually when you really need to question someone, they will just go and sleep all day after you shoot them. It all depends, of course, on where the little dart enters."

Liffey tried not to obviously stare with disbelief at her friend's supposedly mild-mannered father.

Susan had told her that he had a desk job with the FBI in Madison and was some kind of accountant—not a secret agent who went around shooting people with darts from pens like James Bond.

"All right then, Liffey, let's figure out what to do with our friend here and if you don't mind, I have a few questions I'd like to ask you as well."

"To begin with, who *is* this woman?"

"Don't you think it's still too early to surprise them, Jean?" John asked anxiously.

He kept thinking about his mother's warning that girls needed to have advance notice so they could do their hair and put on makeup.

Somehow, he did not think that Liffey would care. He had never noticed any makeup on her face before and her hair had always looked natural—except when she covered it all up with that Irish dance wig, which made her look crazy.

"It's absolutely never, ever, too early in the day to pleasantly surprise someone, dear," Jean replied.

"They will be thrilled to see us!"

Jean coasted into Robert Rivers' newly plowed front driveway and parked her car.

"The moving van won't get here until nine, so let's kidnap them and take everybody out for breakfast! There is a Gray Dog and a Red Rooster in Mineral Point. Your choice, darling!"

John had no idea whatsoever what Jean Rivers was talking about but in the interest of being cooperative and polite, answered, "I guess I'll go with the bird, Jean."

"Lovely, dear."

They walked to the front door and rang the bell.

Liffey went upstairs with Max through the kitchen after she and Harry had pulled Louise into the hallway closet. She wanted to see if Louise had something in her bedroom that might explain her betrayal, even though she was trying not to dwell on why Louise had suddenly turned against her family.

She had been correct about her compulsive father having followed through with his own advice. The hall closet *did* lock and it was roomy and comfortable inside.

Inside the closet, there was a soft mattress, bottles of water and a few packets of crackers with peanut butter. Like it was expected that it would someday be a temporary holding place for unwelcome visitors, or serve as an emergency guest room.

Liffey turned the security systems back on for the second time and was startled when the front doorbell chimed. She looked at the video monitors and was astounded when she saw John Bergman standing on the front porch with her Aunt Jean.

"What are they *doing* here?" she groaned at Max, who was underfoot, busily chewing on his sock.

I look terrible and there's a body in the downstairs hall closet and an FBI agent walking around in his old bathrobe with a tranquilizer dart pen.

I can't just leave them out there waiting, but I don't think I should be just letting them come inside either. It's like inviting someone to come play real espionage games with you. Who knows what is going to happen next?

Liffey had to admit that it was really nice seeing John Bergman again though. Her Aunt Jean, not so much.

She finally decided she would let them in and deal with the consequences later. Besides, she had told Susan all about her friend John and it would be nice to introduce them to each other.

She turned on the entrance way intercom. "Hello! Really good to see you guys!" Liffey said in a low voice.

"You need to pretend that nobody is home right now though, so please walk back to your car looking very disappointed and then drive around the block and park the car behind the garden shed."

"You can easily see the shed from the road behind the house. Walk quickly up to the back door, using the path that runs between the hedges."

"If you see anyone on the roof, take cover in the bushes immediately and I'll figure out something."

"Bye. Can't wait to let you guys in!"

John was startled.

Maybe his mother had been right after all and Liffey was in there now, buying time to do her hair and makeup while they drove around the block.

He would have assured her on the Alaskan cruise that he did not care about such things but the subject had never come up.

This seems like a lot of hoops to have to jump through just so she can rearrange her face, he thought.

Since he went to an all male high school, he had no real insight into girls wearing or not wearing makeup or how a girl acted if a boy would turn up uninvited.

John detected that Jean Rivers seemed a bit put out by Liffey's request too.

"Well, I guess we'll just go and drive around the block and then sneak in the back door," Jean said.

"You never know what Liffey has gotten herself into but I predict we will soon find out."

John smiled, trying not to feel aggravated as they turned around to walk back to the car.

Just after they had moved the pink Cadillac and parked it by the garden shed as directed, a deafening sound erupted and a helicopter came into view. A man dropped down from it, attached to a harness on a rope, directly above Liffey's roof.

They tried to keep close to the bushes as much as possible as they ran to the house. Jean pounded and screamed:"Liffey, help us! Open this door! There's a man dangling above your roof!"

The door opened immediately and Liffey yanked John and her Aunt Jean inside.

"I am going to be in so much trouble for this!"

"Come on, hurry, follow me!"

John was speechless. Was he still on his flight from New Hampshire to Wisconsin? Asleep and dreaming in his window seat?

Before he could make up his mind, Liffey hurried them along with her through the dining room to an open wall panel.

When all three of them had stepped inside what looked like a secret passageway, she pulled a small knob and the wall panel closed.

Liffey then pushed a small button on the wall with blinking green lights that said KITCHEN and a thick steel barrier wall slowly descended from the ceiling, landing with a loud thud, automatically locking in front of the dining room's secret panel.

There was a timer on the lock that flashed red and said, 2400 HOURS. It was ticking.

Liffey turned to John and said, "Welcome back to my life, John." She gave him a big bear hug and said, "Next, I need to secure the garden shed's entrance to the tunnel that leads into the downstairs bathroom." Liffey pushed another button on the wall with the flashing green lights that said: GARDEN SHED. When the button lit up red and began to blink with the 2400 HOURS message, she said, "Good. That's done then. Another steel barrier in place. Nobody is coming through that shed into the tunnel to the

164

bathroom now."

John asked a question that was bothering him. "Liffey, I get the hidden doors and steel barriers, but can't people who really want to get in to your house just break a window?"

"Sure, they could easily get into our above-ground, real house," Liffey readily agreed, "but they cannot get to us in the safe house underground with the three-foot-thick steel barrier doors in place."

"Oops, that reminds me, I need to seal off the garage floor elevator entrance to the living room."

Liffey pushed another button that said, GARAGE FLOOR and a red light blinked on with its 2400 HOURS message, indicating that the horizontal steel floor barrier above the garage elevator platform had moved into place.

"Hello, Aunt Jean!" Liffey finally acknowledged her aunt, who was looking very discombobulated as her niece planted a kiss on her right cheek.

She reached for John's hand and said, "I am not at all sure right now how to tell the good guys apart from the bad guys in this Gray Dog, Red Rooster mess."

"But I am thinking the guy you saw on the rope above us is probably a good guy because the bad guys would probably not be so totally obvious with the helicopter and man-on-the-rope thing," Liffey said, thinking out loud.

"But, just in case I'm wrong, and the man on the rope is *not* a good guy after all, I have sealed us off completely until we can figure everything out."

"I think that John is definitely one of the good guys though, don't you, Aunt Jean?" Liffey smiled and was surprised to feel herself blushing.

John smiled broadly and squeezed her hand.

As the three of them made their way down the spiral staircase and into the safe house's kitchen, he realized that he had no clue as to what was going on here.

Liffey seemed happy to see him though and very much in charge of things, barricading everybody in with steel barriers and not seeming to be bothered much by a strange man dropping down to her roof from a helicopter.

CHAPTER TWENTY-TWO
The Good Guys

Robert Rivers was struggling to maintain some degree of self-control after Liffey told him on the phone that he would not be able to join them in the safe house because it was now on a timer lockdown for the next 24 hours. She tried to explain that she had accidentally pushed the 'Timed Seal' buttons for each of the steel barriers she had lowered instead of the regular 'Seal' ones that would allow the steel barriers to return to their original up positions at anytime.

Liffey used her hush-hush theatrical voice when she told her father that she had heard Louise planting bugs in the living room and kitchen areas early this morning.

"Everything happened so quickly, Daddy. First, I discovered last night that all of our security and surveillance systems had been turned off, which had to mean that for some reason, Louise had turned on us and she is now working against us."

Liffey heard her father on his side of the phone beginning to make loud throat clearing noises like he did when he was too angry to speak.

The last time she had heard him do this was when she had inadvertently closed down the National Portrait Gallery in London after she had told a guard that the Coronation Portrait of Queen Elizabeth I was a forgery and she and her father had both been detained and taken for questioning to New Scotland Yard.

"I am sure you have your reasons to suspect Louise, Liffey, but I need to talk with her right now."

"Sorry, Daddy, but that's impossible."

"Liffey, I am ordering you to put Louise through to me immediately." Liffey could not remember ever hearing her father sound so angry.

"I would totally obey you if I could, Daddy, but," Liffey returned to her hush-hush voice again, "right now she's locked in the hallway closet, unconscious."

The throat-clearing noises on the other side of the phone suddenly became much louder.

Susan, Ann, Maeve, Jean, Harry and John were sitting at the dining room table, pretending to study the codicil but listening intently to Liffey's end of the phone conversation with her father, which was obviously not going well.

After John had gotten used to the idea that there was an unconscious woman locked in the hall closet who had been tranquilized by a dart from a pen used by the skinny dude with thick glasses sitting across from him in a faded blue terrycloth bathrobe, he had relaxed considerably.

"I don't know HOW to undo the steel barrier doors, Daddy. There's a timer on them that started counting down from 2400, for the next twenty-four hours, I am guessing? Are there instructions for the door timers somewhere? Can you hang with the good guys so you're safe?"

"Okay. Okay. Okay. All RIGHT! I'll get mother for you. Bye! Love you, Daddy!"

John Bergman wondered if he might actually be of some use here today as to figuring out the locks on the steel barrier doors.

Liffey handed the phone to her mother with a "geez" grunt and joined the others at the table.

She bowed her head dramatically and said, "Oh well, since I have apparently locked all of us in now, it's a good time to solve this whole codicil thing. We know where the gold mine is located thanks to Susan's memory clicking on and Harry here started to explain to us who the Gray Dog and Red Rooster are and what the Fox and Horse are about before he fell asleep last night. So let's start up again where he left off."

"Without further ado, Ladies and Gentleman, I give you Mister Harry Scott, Master Spy."

"May we please have some applause? And..."

She stopped mid-sentence. *What is wrong with me? I have totally lost it!* she thought, quickly downshifting. I need to divert this conversation immediately.

Aunt Jean spoke up impatiently. "Please excuse me, but does anyone know what time it is? I am meeting my movers at the new house at 9:00 a.m."

Maeve Rivers, who had finally hung up on Robert Rivers after he could only make sputtering noises on the other end, exchanged worried looks

169

with Liffey. "I beg your pardon, Jean? You are meeting movers *where?*" asked Maeve.

Jean smiled broadly and said, "Oh well, I guess now is as good a time as any to let the cat out of the bag! Does anyone know what that actually means? I don't but I must confess that I do use the expression from time to time."

Liffey flashed John, sitting directly across the table, an exasperated look. Sometimes she found her aunt's long-winded chattering totally unendurable.

"Anyway, it's drum roll time! As of today, I am going to be your almost-next-door-neighbor!"

"That's why John is here—to help me move in and, of course, to visit with Liffey."

There was a stuffy silence. Maeve buried her face in her hands and Liffey looked accusatorily at John for confirmation.

"She told me not to ruin the surprise and tell you guys," he whispered defensively.

"Also, I have hair and pedicure appointments in town at 2:00 and 4:00. Afterwards, I thought I'd take us all out for dinner. That is, of course, after Liffey gives John a tour of the Point," Jean gushed.

"Yes! Yes! Yes! Please do tell us all about your new house, Aunt Jean," Liffey practically shouted. "Every single detail! I just cannot wait to see it!"

In spite of her mother's 'if looks could kill' glance, Liffey grabbed a blank sheet of paper and began to scribble a message to the people sitting at the table in large letters:

IMPORTANT!!!

SOS!!! I FORGOT!!!! WE CANNOT TALK ABOUT THE CODICIL BECAUSE LOUISE PLANTED BUGS. I HEARD HER THIS MORNING WALKING AROUND. ALSO, HARRY--SHE PROBABLY HAD THE VIDEO KIND SO WE ARE BEING WATCHED AND EAVESDROPPED ON BY PEOPLE SHE IS WORKING FOR. LANDLINE PHONES ARE PROB BUGGED OR TAPPED TOO. I HAVE EXPERIENCE LOCATING THE VIDEO KIND SO I'LL GET RIGHT ON IT.

Aunt Jean, who had not seemed to notice that Liffey was hastily composing an urgent message to everyone sitting at the table, raced on enthusiastically.

"Well of course you can see my house, Liffey, darling. As soon as your father figures out how to get us out of this fortress, we will all be off in a flash."

"Maeve, darling, I really could use your input on decorating and also to help me arrange a house reading because I think I want to use Feng Shui, to create Sheng Chi and get rid of all the Sha Chi, which brings me back to my original question, what time is it now?"

Enough! Maeve thought. "Jean, it really does not matter what time it is now because none of us are going anywhere soon!"

"You had better call the movers and ask them to

171

unload without you," Ann Scott offered.

Jean looked crushed and confused.

"Do they have a key?" Maeve asked.

"Actually they do. I also drew up a map of where to put each piece of heavy furniture," Jean answered.

John was very relieved to learn that he was not going to be breaking his back moving an entire household of furniture by himself later on today—or whenever they would actually be able to leave these barricaded premises.

"When I signed the contract," Jean began, "they asked for a key in case of an emergency, which I suppose one might call our situation here at the moment."

Liffey was spinning around with out-stretched arms in the kitchen, causing what she said would be "merry-go-round-dizziness-syndrome" if anyone was watching. Ceremoniously, she dropped two button-like objects down on the dining room table that had been planted on kitchen cabinet doors.

Harry smiled, placing the button he had found hidden above the dining room chandelier, next to Liffey's find.

"Cool scavenger hunt," John remarked, plunking down a fourth video button camera.

"Where did you find that one, John?"

"It was on the Skype camera in the computer cubicle," he answered, gathering up all the bugs and placing them inside a kitchen drawer wrapped in layers of dish towels.

"So then," Aunt Jean declared, "you can all see clearly now, how terribly important it is when you are moving into a new house, to clear out all of the Sha Chi first!" No one could disagree.

Liffey closed her eyes, crossed her fingers and said, "So let's start up again where Harry left off last night."

Harry laughed good naturedly and began: "Once upon a time, long ago in BC time, there was a storyteller named Aesop who lived in Greece. We intelligence agents sometimes use his stories to talk with each other in a kind of foreign language. And, as you probably already know, Aesop's tales always have a moral at the end of the story."

"Liffey has already figured out that the codicil has characters from an Aesop's Fable, Pops," Susan said, trying to move Harry up to a faster speed.

"Well, Liffey was absolutely right," Harry said cheerfully. "In your Uncle William's codicil, the dog, the rooster and the fox that is riding on the horse— all these cartoons are players in a bizarre scenario unfolding right now in real time. Much more than a gold mine is at stake—that's why the government agencies are counting on us to get them to that place Susan remembered going to with her Great Uncle William long ago."

"He was relying on me and especially Susan, it seems, to figure it all out, but without Liffey Rivers, I am not at all confident that any of us would have."

Harry paused to sip the coffee in front of him.

173

"Especially since my brother, Tom, is apparently trying to undermine our efforts," Harry said.

Maeve and Ann winced. Tom Scott had been missing since yesterday but Harry did not need to be burdened with that knowledge. The police knew.

"Anyway, Uncle William used an Aesop's Fable about a Rooster, Fox and Dog to get an important message through to me."

"A Fox comes trotting down a road and sees the Rooster sitting up in a tree. The Fox announces that King Lion has declared a universal truce that all the beasts of the earth shall dwell in brotherly friendship.

The Fox only says this because it wants to eat the Rooster and the Rooster sees through this plot and says something like, 'Oh wonderful, I see my friend the Dog coming down the path now. He will be thrilled that we are all living in peace now!'

When the Fox hears this, he starts to run away because he knows the Dog will attack him. When the Rooster reminds him that they are living in brotherly peace now, the Fox expresses his fear that the Dog may not have heard King Lion's decree."

There were confused looks exchanged all around the table. Before anyone could ask a question about what this Aesop Fable's moral actually was, Aunt Jean said, "Please excuse me once again, but does anyone know what time it is?"

Harry said: "The moral of this fable is: cunning often outwits itself." That said, he smiled and began to snore.

CHAPTER TWENTY-THREE
The Bad Guys

A private Gulfstream 650 jet, adorned with bright silver paint and an elaborate Fox and Hounds Society Coat of Arms on both sides, landed in Milwaukee from Beijing, China, fourteen hours after the Society's intelligence had intercepted an e-mail sent from an IP address in Mineral Point, Wisconsin.

A luncheon invitation text from a Susan Scott to her friend at an encrypted address which remained unknown, had contained many key search words and phrases: 'Red, Rooster, Gray, Dog, Fox, William Scott.' Combined with other words in the same text—'codicil, mystery, solve, last will and testament, sleuth,' it seemed relevant. After follow-up revealed that William Scott had died recently in Mineral Point, it was the first solid clue the Society had unearthed as to the likely whereabouts of their stolen property.

Reginald Paddlestone, president of The Fox and Hounds Society's Beijing chapter, exited the plane from inside the hangar he had reserved. He was upbeat about finding the location of his counterfeit money-making paraphernalia which had been stolen by the Red Rooster a year and a half ago from the Club's supposedly impenetrable underground bunker. The Rooster's spoils would soon be discovered and heading back to China where they belonged—in his capable hands.

At first, Mr. Paddlestone could not think of a good reason why the stolen equipment had not been immediately turned over to Scott's U.S. employer—probably the Secret Service.

Eventually, Paddlestone had concluded that it was a brilliant move on Harper's part *not* to turn the equipment over because its whereabouts was his life insurance policy. Paddlestone rarely resorted to harsh punishments, but deliberate treason was treason, and Scott, aka Henry Harper, was a traitor who knew that his theft and defection warranted the death penalty.

It seemed logical that when Harper sensed that his health was spent and death was imminent, he would direct his family to his hoard's location. Scott knew his FBI nephew would oversee the equipment's delivery to the proper authorities. To protect his nephew, he had left obscure cartoon directions to the stash of stolen equipment in a codicil to his will.

William Scott, known in China as the Reverend Henry Harper, had pulled the wool over his eyes for two years before he had disappeared. He had been posturing as a disgruntled, retired British cleric from Leeds who proclaimed regularly that: "The Kingdom of God is at hand. Repent!"

He was considered to be very eccentric but was still highly regarded. Eventually, he was recruited for club membership after six months of socializing with members at local gatherings of mostly British and Irish expatriates who lived in Beijing. He fit in well and soon he was made an officer of the Fox and Hounds Society Beijing Chapter.

After Harper had gained their trust, they had revealed to him the real purpose of the Fox and Hounds Society in Beijing—an elaborate plan to ruin the UK economy by flooding it and other parts of Europe with counterfeit £20 British sterling notes.

"The Nazis had made a feeble attempt to pass counterfeit British notes in the 1940's but had failed miserably," Paddlestone told Harper.

When Henry Harper had asked him why he was so determined to ruin the economy of the UK with counterfeit money, Paddlestone had answered like it was an obvious, stupid question: "Why? Why? Why, for revenge, of course! Because the Crown ruined us many long years ago! It rewarded our steadfast loyalty with the blackest treachery! We have waited almost three hundred years, but the time has finally time for payback!"

Harper, counseling like an authentic clergyman, had suggested that Paddlestone should let bygones be bygones and forgive, but Paddlestone vehemently disagreed.

177

It seemed that Paddlestone's relatives and all of the founding members of the Fox and Hounds Society, had come from England to Ireland with Cromwell to put down the Great Irish Rebellion of 1641. After 11 bitter years of war, England was flat broke. So they paid their victorious army off—not with money but with Irish land, taking it away from the "Irish traitors."

Paddlestone readily admitted that his family had received Irish land as payment and for 70 years his family had lived high on the hog. But then, after the War of the Spanish Succession had ended, England found itself in a depression, and sought to get out of it by passing its problems on to Ireland.

"The fatal blow came," Paddlestone was turning purple during his final analysis of how England had ruined the new gentry in Ireland, "when the English Parliament deliberately sabotaged the Irish currency, causing total ruin to many of the new gentry, we Paddlestones among them."

"For centuries, we have bided our time. As old members of the Fox and Hounds Society fell away, no longer caring what had happened centuries before to their families, they were replaced with others who did care."

"Now Great Britain will experience what an economic collapse feels like. We will create absolute chaos with their sacred currency. Worthless British pounds will move across Europe like an incurable plague."

CHAPTER TWENTY-FOUR
Reflections

John Bergman was thinking how was he ever going to be able to go back home again to his boring life of endless, dreary study halls and tennis. He was still having difficulty trying to figure out exactly what was going on around here at the Rivers' safe house but whatever it was, it sure beat prepping around all day at school and then, after daily tennis practices, studying all night at home. This place was exciting.

Aunt Jean was thinking about how she could not endure even one more minute underground in this gopher hole, worrying about all her furniture and whether the movers were going to let in Sha Chi.

Ann Scott was thinking about whether or not her husband, Harry, was ever going to be able to explain what was actually going on without falling asleep. She was contemplating throwing ice water on him to jog his memory.

Harry Scott was relieved that the authorities were involved with the events unfolding now because he realized he could not hold a thought in his head for more than a few minutes lately. He would have to try to remember to call his doctor to look into changing his prescription drugs.

Maeve Rivers was hoping her husband, Robert, would figure out how to get back into the safe house before tomorrow because she sensed a real urgency in her daughter. Liffey reminded her of a barometer indicating a hurricane was imminent.

Susan Scott was fixated on finding the gold mine and buying some new clothes. Things had been tight at home lately.

Louise Anderson stared into the blackness, munching on peanut butter crackers and sipping Perrier Mineral Water, trying to figure out how a small terrier and a 14-year-old girl had managed to subdue and knock her out and why, after a perfect record of integrity and honesty, she had betrayed the Rivers family in the first place.

She remembered seeing a frail-looking man in a blue bathrobe. He had been holding a pen but he had not come near her. It was infuriating to know that Liffey must have done this all by herself.

Between bites, she methodically tried to pick the hallway closet lock with the emergency tools she had removed from her right shoe when she had regained consciousness.

Only Robert Rivers would have thought to install a night light in a hall closet and make this so easy.

CHAPTER TWENTY-FIVE
Lock Picking

Time was hanging heavily on everybody's hands in the safe house and Liffey had had enough. John told her that he could figure out how most locks worked because he had taught himself how to break into his parents' house several times last summer to test their security systems.

"It drove my father crazy," he said, "but I did it to prove a point—burglars are smart." His father had installed three different systems before John had to admit that he could not figure out how the third one worked. He suggested that there was nothing to lose if Liffey allowed him to have a go at one of the locked timers.

She had to agree. On the pretense of walking Max and allowing him to 'do his business' on the tiled floor in the bathroom off the hallway, Liffey left with John and Max the Magnificent.

They pushed the bathtub away from the wall and entered the hallway that led to the stairs to the garden shed. John went to work on the locked steel barrier at the top of the stairs with his Swiss Army knife while Liffey 'walked' Max at the bottom of the stairs in the tunnel.

"How did you get your knife through security?" she called up the stairs.

"Good question. I have no clue. I forgot that it was in my backpack until I was looking for my phone after I landed."

John asked if Liffey could find him a paper clip. She located her mother's purse on the round table at the end of the hallway and felt around at the bottom. After retrieving a pile of bobby pins, a paper clip appeared, embedded in a tissue. Liffey smiled. It was usually possible to find almost anything you might need in her mother's handbag.

After a few minutes, Liffey could hardly believe her eyes and ears when John disabled the timer and the barrier door lock clicked open.

"You made it look as easy as opening a jammed garage door, John! Should I tell everybody you're a genius?" Liffey was ecstatic.

"Nah, I don't think so. Why bother? Your Aunt Jean is nuts. Harry is sick and exhausted. His wife is way, way too uptight. Susan seems lost in space. Your mom already has enough on her plate and the lady in the hall closet cannot be trusted. Your dad might be homicidal by now, but we'll have to give him a call to tell him that he can get in now."

Louise was almost ready to take control. She could not wait to see the look on Liffey's face when she emerged from the closet holding the mini-gun she had assembled. *So glad I never told Liffey about my special shoes!* she thought.

If everybody just did what she told them to do, no one would get hurt. All her new employer wanted was the return of what had been taken from him and was rightfully his. She had already been paid 500,000 British pounds and she was not about to miss the final half million installment.

Louise slowly opened the door. *No time like the present.* She hoped Max was not going to announce her before she made her entrance.

She smiled as she moved cautiously towards the dining room, where she could hear them discussing the codicil, completely unaware that every word they said was being recorded. She hoped that by now, they had already given away enough information for her employer to have been able to locate and retrieve his stolen property.

She would need to get out of here immediately when she was told "mission accomplished" because she knew that Robert Rivers would be after her with a vengeance. She couldn't blame him.

A flight plan out of the country had been filed using another identity and after she collected the second 500,000 installment as promised, somewhere in Mineral Point at a dead drop location, she would drive to Dubuque, Iowa, where she had bought a plane that she would pilot herself to the islands.

The detective agency's corporate jet she had flown to Rockford International Airport had already been sold at a bargain price to people who did not ask any questions.

She had never planned on an early retirement, but then, she had also never planned to receive one million British pounds either—almost two million

U.S. dollars when the dollar's value was down.

Besides, she was tired of the cloak and dagger routine in her life and was ready to become a full-time beach bum. She had saved money over the years and along with this new windfall, she should have enough to last her for a very long time.

Louise moved slowly from the hallway into the dining room where she was greeted with alarmed, startled expressions.

"Hello Harry Scott, Susan Scott, Maeve Rivers, Jean Rivers, Ann Scott and...Liffey?"

"Where is Liffey?" Louise asked sharply, backing against the far dining room wall to include a view of the hallway.

"Hello, Louise," Maeve Rivers said shortly. "At first I had difficulty believing my daughter when she told me you had turned against us. I hoped that it was her over-active imagination and that when you woke up we would all have a good laugh. I guess she got it right after all."

For a brief moment, before Louise regained her self-assurance, a look of remorse clouded her face. "I'm afraid Liffey got it right, Maeve."

"Got what right, Maeve?" Aunt Jean asked.

"Have I missed something here?"

CHAPTER TWENTY-SIX
Gray Dogs

Gray Dog was busy gnawing on the large beef bone that the blacksmith, James James, had given him, when he heard the clapping.

After saying two more *Aves* for her dead cousin, Jane clapped her hands commandingly and waved the hambone high above her head. When she reached the back fence, Gray Dog, picking up on the ham scent, got up sniffing and stretching.

"Here, Gray Dog. You come along with me now. See here, I have a juicy ham bone for you."

Gray Dog dropped the depleted beef bone and followed obediently. She continued to hold the ham bone above her head, even though it was hard to do while holding her satchel and the slate with the lovely writing in her free hand, until Mr. Heaton's school came into view.

Before going inside, she patted his head and said, "Good boy. You stay under this big tree, Gray Dog." She put the large bone inside the dog's expectant mouth and hurried inside.

At first recess, Jane carried the old bucket that Mr. Lacey, the substitute teacher filling in for Mr. Heaton, had found in the mud room, out to the water pump. She filled it up to the brim.

Mr. Lacey studied the writing on the slate Jane timidly showed him while Gray Dog slurped up the water from the bucket. He said it made no sense whatsoever. The letters were well executed, but they

185

were all capitals. "A real word might begin with a capital letter," he said, "but this word is made up of only capital letters."

When Jane had asked him what it meant, he had said: "This is not an English word, Jane. Look at the mark above the letter 'A.' Sounded out, the letters, say 'SLAN,' which is not a proper English word. The mark above the 'A' might change the pronunciation of the word, like when the French use a similar *accent aigu* mark to make an 'E' sound like an 'A'." Jane was trying her best to follow Mr. Lacey but she was hopelessly lost.

"Whoever wrote this is ignorant and illiterate like most of you Irish here in Mineral Point."He handed the slate back to Jane and turned crisply on his heel like a foot soldier. Jane felt tears beginning to well up inside but stopped them. She was not about to give Mr. Lacey the satisfaction of seeing her Irish tears.

Gray Dog chewed on the ham bone until Jane came back hours later and clapped her hands again for him to follow. The sting from Mr. Lacey's words about 'ignorant and illiterate Irish' weighed heavily on her heart as she walked home, praying that Mrs. Gibbons' birds were going to be in their coops.

Mam was waiting for her at the front gate. After Jane had explained finding Gray Dog on William's grave, Mam said nothing and walked back into the house.

Jane waited anxiously and said three *Aves*, not at all sure what to expect. She had brought a stray dog

186

home with her *and* had defaced a kitchen chair. When Mam returned from the house with a large piece of beef jerky in her outstretched hand, Jane sighed with relief. Gray Dog had a new home.

Some FBI operative I am, Harry thought, helplessly watching Louise pointing a gun at his family. *Agent Gray Dog doesn't bother checking the lady's shoes because he can't seem to remember how to do anything right anymore.*

Liffey and John and Max were half way down the stairs when Liffey felt the pins and needles stabbing at her again. Max began to growl quietly.

"John, there's something wrong down there," she whispered, taking off her ankle sock and handing it to Max, who stopped snarling and began chewing.

"Okay, let me go ahead and scout. I'll be right back," John volunteered.

Before Liffey could object, they heard Louise demanding to know where "Liffey" was. A slight chill passed through her. Somehow Louise had managed to get out of the hall closet.

"She must be armed, John, or somebody would be moving around down there," Liffey said.

"Liffey, she doesn't even know I'm here," John replied. "Maybe I can throw her off balance by just casually walking into the room."

"And then what?" Liffey sighed.

"How would she have gotten a gun? Didn't you

and Harry search her before you dragged her into the closet?" John asked.

Liffey hated to admit that she and Harry had not done that.

"Well, you should have!" he exclaimed.

"Duh!" Liffey said, "but it's a bit late now for a lecture, don't you think?"

"I'm sorry, it's amazing what you've done so far," John said, placing his hands on her shoulders and brushing her forehead with a brief kiss.

"Look, we can do this together. I'll just walk in cheerfully like I don't see her gun or whatever she's using to control everybody. Nobody would have told her that I'm here."

"No, John. We need to think about this for a minute."

Hoping John would not take notice, she bent down to the ground and picked up the 'Imaginary Thinking Cap' her dad had taught her to put on her head when she felt at her wits end. It was a trick she had used since early childhood to calm herself down while she tried to put scary things back into the right perspective before taking action.

"Louise is going to be furious if she discovers that we've dismantled and hidden all of her video surveillance buttons. She probably thinks she has directions to the gold mine by now but all she's got is Max biting her ankles and me sitting on her chest. Oh—and Harry totally saving me with his magic pen. Let's go back up to the garden shed and wait outside.

My dad is probably on his way here now with the entire Army Corps of Engineers. Please tell me you've got your phone!"

Robert Rivers was driving towards Mineral Point from Madison trying not to fixate on the fact that his family was now locked inside the safe house he had personally designed and supervised with no way out. Not to mention the fact that no one could get in from the outside either.

This was not the way a safe house was supposed to work. Everything was going wrong.

He had expected to return last night but had been delayed—twice. He told the Interpol and FBI agents staked out at his house that Louise Anderson was locked inside a closet now and should, for the time being anyway, still be considered armed and dangerous. Talks had begun on what the best way would be to cut through one of the steel barriers.

A disturbing thought crossed his mind. He had forgotten to tell someone about the gun that he knew Louise always carried in her left shoe.

Before he could dwell on this potential wrinkle, his phone rang. Not recognizing the number, he was surprised and confused to hear his daughter's voice instead.

"Daddy, I'm so sorry I was such a brat this morning when I told you about how I accidentally locked everybody in here. Do you remember John Bergman from the cruise ship last spring? Well, he's here with me now and he popped the lock on the steel barrier outside the dining room with a paper clip from mom's purse, so that's done, but we really need to do something soon about Louise because she's totally not working for us anymore and I'm thinking she must have a gun aimed at everybody as we speak because it's way too quiet down there."

Robert Rivers tried to make words come out of his mouth. Had his daughter really said all that in one breath?

He needed to tell Liffey that the 'good guys,' as she called them, had been plotting to get in and that he would tell them that it was now possible.

But all he could manage to say was, "I thought Louise was locked in the hall closet?"

"She *was*, Daddy, but she must have escaped and, like I said, I am almost certain she has a gun aimed at everyone. I heard her demanding to know where I was a few seconds ago when John and I were going back down the stairs to tell everyone about the lock."

Attorney Rivers felt pole-axed.

He was drowning with guilt when he thought again about how he had neglected to tell Maeve, or anyone else for that matter, about how Louise kept emergency tools in her shoes along with a miniature gun.

Stunned by Liffey's report of the deteriorating circumstances in the safe house, the only words he heard tumbling out from his mouth were, "What is John Bergman doing in Mineral Point?"

CHAPTER TWENTY-SEVEN
Plotting

It seemed obvious to Liffey that if they, meaning herself, John, her family and the Scotts, were ever going to regain control over this safe house situation, they must move quickly to subdue Louise again.

Since she and John were not in the room where everyone else was being held at gunpoint, it was up to them to figure something out.

Even though Liffey knew there were people on the roof who could help, she feared that if she or John ran outside to get that help, the agents might launch a rescue mission and Louise might actually shoot at someone.

Something unexpected needed to happen.

"John, I think I might have to go down there and take my chances. First though, I need to call ahead. Maybe I can fix everything from right here."

John looked skeptical and worried.

"Actually," Liffey continued, thinking out loud, "I need to talk briefly, or at least get a message through to Harry because it's entirely possible that Louise has not yet realized who it was that finally took her down."

"First it was Max, then me, then came Harry's dart pen. I am so hoping she does not know about Harry's pen. But if you think about it, the dart came from a small, regular-looking ball point pen and the entry point would have been almost invisible."

"I had to do a body search to remove the dart. I found it in her left shoulder and it was no bigger than a small tip of a tack. She may very well be clueless as to how she ended up in the hall closet. Somehow, I need to tell Harry that if he does have another dart, he needs to shoot it at Louise again."

"He's not in the greatest mental shape at the moment and he might have forgotten that he still has another dart or two in his pen," Liffey concluded.

"Sounds like an idea," John agreed. "However, I don't want you going down there and risking her wrath if this phone call does not work."

"That's why I need to talk to my mother. Louise will probably let her talk to me just so things seem normal. Remember, Louise thinks she's still being videotaped and will want to show 'them,' whoever 'them' might be, how she's in total control of everything. You wait—I am betting she will order my mom to ask me where I am."

"It's worth a try," John agreed as Liffey dialed her mother's number.

The small, nervous group sitting at the octagon table jumped nervously when Maeve's phone began to vibrate.

"Pick it up, Maeve, and do not say anything rash or you will regret it," Louise ordered icily.

Maeve tried to remain calm as she reached for the phone on the table.

"Hello. Liffey? Where have you been? I've been worried sick about you. Where are you? Pen? Are you okay? What do you mean you're in **PEN**-darvis? I thought it closed for the season yesterday? Oh, I see. Hmm…"

"Yes, I will ask Harry if he still has his pen handy so he can take things down." Maeve looked at Harry. She was beginning to see where Liffey was going with the pen.

Louise rolled her eyes. "Look guys, I know very well that Liffey is in this house—like the rest of us, locked in. You tell Liffey she had better stop playing games and get herself back in here immediately or there will be consequen…" Louise's voice trailed off as she slumped down to the floor.

"It worked, Liffey!" Maeve was ecstatic.

"Harry got your drift. She's out cold again. John and you can do the honors of pulling her back to the closet—this time without her shoes. She must keep small tools in them."

When Liffey returned to the dining room with John, she considered getting the agents on the roof involved with permanently removing Louise from the premises but she thought that her dad, who said he was only ten minutes away about five minutes ago, might want to have a private word with Louise before she was officially taken into custody.

The instant after John and Liffey had transported shoeless Louise back to the hall closet, Robert Rivers called John.

"That's very good news, but I don't think we need that kind of muscle help anymore." Before John could explain why, Robert Rivers ended the call.

"I think we might be about to receive some company," John said, "and I mean a *lot* of company."

Liffey groaned.

Seconds later, thundering feet were running down the stairs from the garden shed and into the tunnel leading to the bathroom.

"So *who's* coming down here? It sounds like an invading army," Liffey said, rushing back to join the others sitting around the octagon table.

When camouflaged figures raced out from the bathroom pointing their automatic weapons, Maeve grasped Liffey's right hand tightly. John held her left.

Aunt Jean passed out, crumpling down in her chair. John tried to keep her upright with his free hand.

Ann Scott shrieked and reached for Susan who had started to hyperventilate.

Harry took out the pen from his pocket in case he needed to use it again.

John cheered with delight while Max breathed loudly, sleeping underneath the table.

After Mr. Paddlestone had briefed his new team of disgruntled UK expatriates and assorted sympathetic Americans in a back room at the Gray Dog Deli in downtown Mineral Point, it was time to stake out the

Rivers' house. Louise was now MIA. She had not delivered anything useful by way of information other than the location of the safe house.

With her out of the picture, it was impossible to know if the Scotts had figured out the location of the gold mine.

Since there were now people crawling all over the Rivers' grounds, Paddlestone tried his best to remain focused, in spite of the difficulties that lay before him. This mission was sacred to him and he had to stay on course—no matter what.

After he had issued an 'Alert!' this morning to club members who lived within a 150 mile radius of Mineral Point, ten men and four women had arrived, eager to hunt for gold for themselves and the stolen counterfeiting equipment that would put the UK in its proper place—at the very bottom of the heap of bankrupt countries in Europe.

Paddlestone had ended his briefing speech with what he thought was one of his best ever quotes from the Bible: "The Fox and Hounds Club will show the UK that, like *Proverbs* says: "Pride goeth before a fall." He had learned over the years that quoting the Bible made him seem trustworthy and admirable.

Thanks to the Red Rooster's nephew, Tom Scott, who had had no qualms about betraying his family and rounding up all of the hard copies of his uncle's codicil from his brothers and his uncle's attorney's office, Paddlestone was confident that he would soon be digging with little or no interference. It was unlikely that the agents at the Rivers' safe house would be able to mobilize for some time. They would have to clear any action they intended to take with their superiors—a time consuming tradition among governmental agencies.

Heavy earth moving equipment, which would be driven by the scout on the water tower, was parked a block away, waiting for the go ahead.

The problem thus far had been: go where?

He and his group had been ready to move out for over an hour now. He had promised to pay them well for their time and expertise.

Paddlestone always enjoyed paying the people who helped the 'cause' huge sums of money with his counterfeit British pounds.

It amazed him how no one ever seemed to think it was peculiar that he carried so much money around on his person.

He called them his "Paddle Pounds."

CHAPTER TWENTY-EIGHT
Camouflage

Liffey watched the camouflaged people rushing to the hall closet and removing Louise, who was still out cold, like there was some kind of national emergency going on.

Maeve guided their 'rescuers' down to the end of the long hallway into her bedroom where Louise was placed on a bed. Ann and Harry followed.

When Liffey saw that Aunt Jean was waking up, she grabbed Susan's arm and signaled to John, who was watching the drama unfold standing on a dining room chair, to get down.

"The three of us need to get out of here now if we are going to beat whoever it was that hired Louise to locate the gold mine site."

"But Liffey," Susan cut in, "if only *we* know where it is, and the listening bugs were destroyed, even though there was nothing on them about the gold, how would whoever *they* are be able to get there before us? They would have to *follow* us, right?"

"I really hate logic, Susan. I'll think about that question when this is all over."

"Aunt Jean, maybe you can still make your hair appointment if we move quickly," Liffey said.

Aunt Jean perked up immediately.

"Where did you park, John? In back by the shed,

right?" John nodded.

"Great! All right then. Let's find our coats and go!" Liffey could feel the adrenaline surging through her. She wanted to run a mile.

"Come on Aunt Jean," Liffey whispered in her aunt's ear, "we are going to make sure you get to your new stylist." *Eventually*.

John found their coats in the hall closet and before anyone could think of objecting again, Liffey led the group into the bathroom where the door to the tunnel remained open.

Susan still thought that they should wait and go with the adults.

"What is your problem, Susan?" Liffey asked irritably.

"And just what do think the three of us are going to be able to do?" Susan asked sarcastically.

"I'm not stupid, Susan. We will hide and scope the place out and obviously call in my father and his band of merry federal agents and give them the exact location."

"Then why not just wait until your dad gets here and go with him?" Susan insisted.

"Because he would totally *never* let us come along even though we are the ones who figured everything out. Only you know where you were when the forked stick went crazy and scraped your hands, Susan. You will be able to save hours and hours of manpower. My dad and his friends would dig up that entire ridge looking…"

"You *do* remember where the right section of the ridge is, don't you?" Liffey suddenly asked.

Susan looked stricken. "It was a long time ago, Liffey, and…oh well. I'll definitely be grounded for the rest of my life, but let's go try."

Liffey grabbed her aunt's hand and followed John and Susan into the tunnel. They had to be on their way before her mother came looking for them or worse, Robert Rivers arrived—which could be any minute now as Liffey well knew.

When they reached the garden shed, Aunt Jean told the group that she could not make up her mind which hair color she should select at the salon today. "It's an unfamiliar colorist and I am terrified that things might go wrong," she confided.

John and Susan tried not to laugh when Liffey commented, "I know just how you must feel, Aunt Jean. You can't *really* trust a colorist until after they've ruined your hair a few times and finally get it right."

"Okay then. Listen up everybody," Liffey said, shifting gears. "As soon as I open the shed's door, John goes out first—which reminds me, you *do* have the car keys in the purse you're carrying, right, Aunt Jean?" Liffey could not believe that she had forgotten to ask this important question before they had left the house.

"Of course I have the keys in my purse, Liffey. Where else *could* they be?" she asked indignantly, handing the keys over to John.

Liffey continued her instructions. "John, when

199

you get to the car, unlock it manually with the key in the front door so there's no beeping going on and then quickly climb over the front seat to the back and keep down."

"Susan, you go next. Don't open another door. Go to the front seat and then climb in the back with John."

"Aunt Jean, the door will still be open on the driver's side for you. I'll go before you and slide over to the front passenger's seat. John, you will hand me the keys to give to my aunt."

"Then, when we are all in place, Aunt Jean, you will back up and drive at a normal speed, understand? A *normal* speed. Not too fast and not too slow."

Liffey saw that her aunt's hands were trembling.

"Aunt Jean, are you okay with this?" Liffey asked gently. Jean Rivers did not answer.

"John, you're a year older than me so you already have your learner's permit, right? And if there is a licensed driver over 21 in the car, you can legally drive?"

"I guess so," John said, "not really though. In New Hampshire you don't get a learner's permit before you get your regular license. You just have to be 15 ½ and only drive with someone over 25."

"Do you think you can drive us?" Liffey asked hopefully.

"Absolutely," he answered confidently.

Liffey was afraid to ask if he actually *was* 15 ½. She suspected he was not but it was obvious that

Aunt Jean could not collect her nerves enough to drive them anywhere safely and Liffey knew that she herself would be 100% illegal if she drove.

Aunt Jean gratefully moved over to the front passenger's seat as Liffey climbed into the back seat with Susan, and John climbed into the driver's seat.

The Paddlestone volunteer who was still stationed at the top of the city water tower, a block away from the Rivers' house, texted that there was a large pink Cadillac moving away from the grounds.

There appeared to be three women and a young man, who was driving, inside the vehicle. He also reported that it did not look like the 3-person swat team on the Rivers' roof had noticed that the car had left as no one had changed position or appeared to be interested.

Paddlestone's alert scout next texted: *This is Delta Force. Targets spotted. Caravan: activate radio transmitters and standby for further instructions.*

Delta Force? Mr. Paddlestone shook his head and decided that people here in America watched far too much television.

"You do realize, Liffey," said John as the party set out, "that if we are seen leaving, they might try to intercept us and make us lead them to the mine?"

"We have made it relatively simple for them since we are, after all, in a pink Cadillac, advertising where we are every second," he pointed out.

"I know, John, but what choice did we have?"

"Well, they are going to get us sooner than later if we stay in this car, Liffey. I suppose we could ditch the car and walk when we're about a mile away from that barn. It's in the high forties today, and Susan says there's a bike trail part of the way to the barn we could take to avoid being seen."

Susan cut in: "We are almost at County Trunk O where we need to turn left. It's now or never. We need to make a decision fast because we will be out in the open as soon as we turn on to O. John, you will need to make this Caddy fly if we are going to outrun them. Assuming of course, whoever *they* are actually exist," she added.

"Excuse me, John, darling, but I think we are driving away from town and I am certain that my colorist's salon is the other way," Aunt Jean said with considerable alarm.

"Aunt Jean you are so totally right. John, please turn into the Kwik Trip just ahead of us on the right and park. I need to run inside for a second."

"Aunt Jean, I will be right back."

"Susan, use your phone and get on Google Earth Maps starting at County Road O ahead. Try to find the New Baltimore Barn's exact location before we set off."

"Shouldn't we keep moving?" John asked, trying to mask the concern in his voice.

"Trust me," Liffey said as she jumped out of the

car and ran into the Kwik Trip looking for Dustin Fields, a local sculptor she had met at a gallery who worked at the Kwik Trip for rent money.

After Liffey had given cheerful, "no questions asked Dustin," a hundred dollar bill and explained what she had in mind, he was more than happy to be of assistance.

She called her father and told him she would meet up with him on County Trunk O at the NEW BALTIMORE 1838 barn and disconnected the call before Robert Rivers could start interrogating her and order her to return to the house immediately.

She called her mother with other instructions.

"Okay! Everybody but Aunt Jean gets out of this car because the rest of us are changing vehicles," Liffey announced, opening the Cadillac's back door for Susan and the driver's door for Dustin to take over from John, who could not hide his confusion.

"Aunt Jean, this is Dustin. Dustin, this is my aunt, Jean Rivers. He's going to drive you to your hair appointment—eventually, and then take you to your new house to check up on things."

"We will meet you at your house later and switch cars with him in a few hours. He'll help you start unpacking until we show up with his car. He's a really talented sculptor, Aunt Jean, so he can definitely help you with your Feng Shui concerns."

Before Aunt Jean could protest, Liffey slammed the car door shut and Dustin blasted out of the Kwik Trip, heading back to Mineral Point's commercial district, in the hot pink Cadillac.

She grabbed Susan and John's hands and pulled them along with her to the back of the building.

"How in the world did you manage that Liffey?" Susan asked, as the three of them quickly got in to Dustin's black Ford Escort in the rear parking lot.

"I gave him the hundred dollar bill that I always keep in my shoe for emergencies. I remembered he worked the early shift and thankfully, he was about ready to clock out anyway and was happy to help."

"I asked him to humor my aunt and told him I would give him another bill when I get to an ATM."

"This car-switching should give us a few extra minutes for us to outrun whoever it is that might be following us," John said. "Good thinking, Liffey."

"Actually, I thought even better, John. Dustin is going back to the house where Maeve and Ann are waiting in our garage to take Susan and my places in the backseat of the Caddy, so it will have one young man and three females again."

"Then, he is going to drive toward Dodgeville on back roads—in the opposite direction from the New Baltimore Barn. Hopefully the wild goose chase will work and give us some time to meet up with my dad before whoever they are figures out they are way off course."

"Well then, let's go!" John shouted, revving up the engine and peeling out of the Kwik Trip heading southwest.

Ten seconds later, Dustin's Ford Escort turned

left on to County Trunk O traveling straight South with no cars in pursuit.

"We can ditch the car a few miles ahead on the Cheese Trail," Susan said.

John and Liffey exchanged 'huh?' looks.

"We'll turn left when we get to Tibbets Road, then immediately right on to the bike trail. The trail crosses right over Tibbets Road the instant we turn. We'll take the trail until it turns away from O—which conveniently happens to be not too far from the New Baltimore Barn!"

"Whew!" John exclaimed. "It's a bike trail then? I was afraid to ask you what a cheese trail in Wisconsin might be."

"What about all the melting snow," Liffey asked, "how can we drive through all the mud?"

"The bike trail will be graveled," Susan answered. "I think."

The lookout man on the water tower texted the others that the pink car had reversed its direction and was now headed back into town on Business 151. He advised the caravan to make sure their phones were turned on.

A few seconds later, he texted: *Caddie possibly heading back to target house. Stand by.*

Maeve Rivers, although furious with Liffey for having snuck off, answered Liffey's call from the Kwik Trip and was ready to move out with Ann Scott. She listened for a toot from the driveway that would alert her to open the garage door.

When the Cadillac arrived, the ladies hopped into the back seat and slumped down a bit to look smaller.

Dustin Fields backed the car out and headed northeast, turning on to County Road PD, paralleling Highway 151.

When Maeve told Jean Rivers they were acting as decoys so the authorities could eventually follow the people who would be following the Cadillac, Aunt Jean replied, "Decoys are wooden ducks. I think what you really meant to say is that we are creating a diversion, Maeve."

Maeve sighed. How could her husband's sister be so smart sometimes when she normally seemed as thick as a brick?

The man on the water tower texted one more update: *Pink Caddy now heading out of town on back road paralleling 151. Heading northeast. Prepare to pursue. Target out of visual range. Delta Force, signing out.*

CHAPTER TWENTY-NINE
A Bit Off

Things felt a 'bit off' to Reginald Paddlestone. He was facing some significant, unanticipated problems.

He had not factored in that most, if not all of the volunteer Fox and Hounds Society zealots in the United States would be carrying legal guns and were probably itching for a shootout of some sort today.

He had inadvertently provided the opportunity for these Americans to let their bullets fly—or do whatever it was that bullets do. He hated guns. There were other, much more inventive ways to get the upper hand. Any idiot could buy and shoot a gun.

All he wanted was the equipment William Scott had stolen from him.

If there was a gold mine, fine.

If not, who cared?

Certainly not himself.

He did not want or need it.

Aside from his concern about guns…there was something else.

He smelled trickery.

His latest update from the water tower sentinel had the pink Cadillac monstrosity going out of town, possibly headed to the gold mine site.

Possibly not.

The word 'diversion' popped into his head and it occurred to him that perhaps his faithful band of 'Delta Force' volunteers might now be following the wrong car.

He really needed to listen to Louise Anderson's surveillance tapes but the fact that he had heard nothing from her in such a long time did not bode well.

Something bad had to have happened or she would have been back in touch long ago.

He feared the worst but smiled because his tower scout had told him that there were camouflage-attired troops of some sort swarming all over the Rivers' grounds.

I can do that, he thought, popping his SUV's trunk open. *One must always travel with several wardrobe changes, should one have to change unexpectedly.*

Within minutes, Mr. Paddlestone was outfitted in universal camouflage attire and driving to the Rivers' bunker.

The time had come to sort things out firsthand.

The tension between Robert Rivers and Louise was palpable. The Interpol agents now present in the safe house were downcast because they had worked with Louise on the Alaskan Sun cruise ship when she had been employed by the Rivers family to protect them.

Now things had been turned upside down and questioning her was very awkward.

Louise sat, hands bound in front of her and

barefoot, at the dining room table.

So far, she had declined to answer any questions. She maintained that she knew nothing because she had been unable to listen to or watch the surveillance tapes.

"You mean these, Louise?" Robert Rivers asked, dropping the surveillance bugs John had given him on to the table. Louise did not try to hide her look of amazement.

"You wouldn't have found anything of use on them anyway, Louise. Liffey warned everyone not to discuss anything important in the common areas because she watched you sneaking around in the dark like a freakin' tooth fairy, planting these."

"Then, after Harry here showed you his special agent moves, you were put into the hall closet for the first time."

"Your little spy toys had already been dismantled by the time you woke up—the first time," Robert Rivers added, turning around and abruptly walking out of the room, overcome with emotion.

Mr. Paddlestone listened intently from the back of the hallway. So Louise had failed. He was glad he had paid her with counterfeit money.

Paddlestone had heard enough.

Just as he had expected, he blended in easily with the local National Guardsmen—so long as he kept his British-accent mouth shut and so far, it had not been a problem.

He passed by Robert Rivers who was animatedly

talking with his wife in the bathroom.

They would be mortified to discover that I am right here in their midst! I need to get out of here presto to contact the parade following the pink car and get them regrouped.

He was delighted to see that there was no one posted by the back door and walked quickly out of the garden shed and over to his SUV parked across the street.

He cheerfully waved good bye to the swat team on the roof who saluted back.

How could this have been so easy?

He called the water tower man with the new instructions and pulled down the block to wait for Robert Rivers to leave the house on a pretense of some sort.

He was fairly certain that Mr. Rivers would not want the guns and enthusiastic troops involved.

Rivers would leave with the special agents who would be elite professionals and much easier to deal with than the locals.

Although he could not be certain, he suspected that Rivers knew the location of the mine because when he had heard him talking with his wife in the bathroom, she had said that Liffey had just run off with the Scott girl. He would soon be going after his daughter.

Five minutes later, two dark blue, late model Ford Crown Victoria sedans sped by the SUV. Obviously government cars with darkened windows.

Paddlestone told the up-in-the-tower recruit to

210

standby with the earth movers and took off after Robert Rivers and the agents, keeping a carefully measured distance.

He would launch the small drone in the back of his SUV out in the country when they had led him to the location.

It would give him coordinates and site photos and as soon as he had those, he would manually fly it in the opposite direction from his SUV and terminate its mission.

Hopefully, it would distract his enemies when he pressed the 'self-destruct' button.

Then, in the midst of the organized confusion, he would dispatch his cowboys to apprehend the agents, march them away, tie them up and keep them under guard while he and a few other volunteers retrieved his stolen property.

After he had loaded the equipment into the U-Haul truck one of the volunteers had donated for the cause, he would drive immediately to the airplane hangar in Milwaukee where his pilots were already prepping his plane for the return flight to Beijing.

He hoped his idiot volunteer army would keep their mouths shut after they located his property and loaded it into his truck, even though he didn't really care one way or another.

They had no information that would lead to him or to his inner circle.

They were morons.

He would leave a pile of Paddle Pounds behind

and let them use the bogus money until they were caught with it. The local banks, not being used to handling British pounds—real or otherwise, would probably notify the authorities immediately.

Some of his volunteers would certainly end up in jail. But by that time, he would be landing in China.

He was not in a good mood.

This field operation was taking far too long.

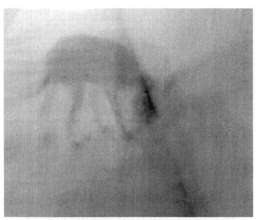

CHAPTER THIRTY
November 1, 1843

Da worked in the lead mines when he could find the work and Patrick filled in for him at home on the farm.

Since Patrick had never much liked attending school and had developed a keen interest in developing a produce business, it was a satisfactory arrangement.

Ever since he and Da had not been able to hunt Passenger pigeons last year after the hanging, Patrick had thought about the possibility of growing more crops than his family actually needed for themselves and selling the surplus over in Mineral Point.

He knew first-hand that there was seldom any good, fresh food available in the Point.

Most of the miners were used to putting up with rice, treacle, bread and coffee for every meal.

If he were to plant a potato patch in back of the

213

barn and grow cabbages, carrots, turnips and onions on some of their uncultivated acres, he might make enough money to fix up the barn and purchase a second milking cow and a few more chickens.

He could sell the surplus milk and eggs.

Jane Scott was still grieving for the loss of Gray Dog. For almost the entire year following the hanging, it seemed like he had fit right in with the family.

He slept by the hearth, played catch in the fields with her, chased rabbits, caught snakes.

Then, just when things seemed to be all natural and happy, he ran off.

After three days of searching, Jane finally found him.

She had checked William Caffee's grave before and after school every day since Gray Dog took off because she always had a hunch he would go back there when it was his own time to pass on.

So it made perfect sense to Jane that he had returned to the grave on November 1, 1843, on the one-year anniversary of his master's death.

Like she had promised her cousins last year, Jane gathered up Black-Eyed Susans and late blooming Queen Anne's Lace she found growing in the fields alongside the road. She laid the large yellow and white bouquet on William Caffee's grave, next to his faithful dog.

Many of the wild flowers she had planted in the

spring were thriving and had overtaken the invasive weeds and crabgrass back in the untended part of the cemetery.

Gray Dog licked her hand but did not accept the bone Mam had given her to bribe him home again if she found him.

Instead, when Jane sat down, he laid his head on her lap and closed his eyes.

She remained with Gray Dog for hours, skipping school, like she had one year ago today, until the weary dog sighed, opened his eyes, looked directly up at her and quietly passed.

She did not want to leave Gray Dog for the carrion birds, so she held him close and waited.

When the sun began to dip low in the sky, she saw her family's wagon coming around the corner.

Patrick got down and hitched the horse to the cemetery's wrought iron fence.

"Let's take Gray Dog home now, little nipper," he said, awkwardly patting her head.

Jane smiled through her tears.

"I think Gray Dog would most likely want to stay right where he is, Patrick, don't you?"

"I thought you might say that," he answered, walking back to the wagon.

The sun had left the sky when Patrick shoveled the last dirt on Gray Dog's grave where he rested a few feet above his master.

"Slán, Gray Dog," Jane murmured through her tears, rearranging the flowers she had brought earlier today for William Caffee on top of their common grave.

She closed her eyes as the wagon set off, fondly recalling the day she had brought Gray Dog home with her and how Mam had given him the beef jerky and how Mam had never mentioned the writing on the chair until she had told her months later what Mr. Lacey had said about the ignorant, illiterate Irish in Mineral Point.

"Is that so now? Well, Missy, I am the one who is after writing those beautiful letters on the slate to say a proper, fancy farewell to your cousins," Mam had shocked her with.

"They never returned to the house so they never saw the 'farewell' word I had written in Irish and set out for them next to their tea and bread. When I went out to fetch them in from the barn, they had already left and I forgot to erase your slate when I placed it next to your school satchel before I was off to visit with poor Mrs. O'Hare.

Jane sighed contentedly. Since their conversation, her mam had taught her to write many Irish words and Jane had taught her mam how to write many useful words in English.

It had been quite a year for the Scott family.

CHAPTER THIRTY-ONE
New Baltimore Barn

John Bergman was racing along on County Trunk O trying to dodge the deep puddles created by the rapidly melting snow. The surrounding farm fields looked like large pans of fudge brownies dusted with powdered sugar.

"Slow down, John!" Susan shrieked.

County O looked like a twisty straw, snaking up and down little hills with sharp bends in the road. "Please! Slow down Mr. Toad! Enough already!" Liffey begged.

It was obvious to both girls that John did not have much experience behind the wheel of a car because he was driving irresponsibly fast on a slick surface with patches of snow and streams of water.

John complied and slowed down some, pointing out that they were, after all, being pursued.

Liffey counter-pointed-out that so far, there had been no sign of anyone following them and that was because whoever might think they were pursuing them, would actually be following her aunt's pink Cadillac, not this Ford Escort.

"My apologies, ladies," John said. "I got carried away. You have to admit though, the past several hours have seemed more like an action movie than real life, and the high speed chase thing just seemed like a logical plot development."

"Also…," his voice trailed off as he looked in the rearview mirror, "I really hate to be the bearer of bad tidings, but there are two large dark cars about a mile behind us," John said warily. "How far away is that cheese trail, Susan?"

"Tibbets Road should be coming up anytime now," she replied, consulting her satellite map.

"It's entirely possible that we have not been seen yet," Liffey pointed out hopefully. "There are so many dips in this road and enough distance…"

"There it is!" Susan interrupted. "Turn left on Tibbets, then turn right immediately on to the bike trail."

John did as instructed. He could see that the trail still had at least two inches of melting snow on it, but as Susan had thought, it was not muddy because it was surfaced with gravel.

"I think we should stop ahead in that clump of high bushes and trees up ahead and formulate our plan," Liffey said. "Even though the leaves are mostly gone, it looks like there is enough ground cover to hide us."

John parked the Escort just off the bicycle trail, underneath a maze of intertwining tree branches.

After a brief discussion, the group agreed that they were going to have to wing it and decided to set out again. Susan would tell them when they needed to leave the trail when it eventually turned away from O and then they would have to walk.

Mid-conversation, two dark blue cars with tinted windows sped by on O past the hidden Escort.

Before John started up the car again for the last part of their journey to the New Baltimore Barn, a speeding SUV passed. After Liffey counted to 100 to put some space between the Escort and SUV, they returned to the trail.

"Like I have already said, the bike trail is going to turn away before we get to the New Baltimore Barn," Susan remarked, "but we should be able to make our way across the fields easily. They will be muddy and gross but so what!"

"It will only be about a half mile walk back over to County Road O and the BARN!" Susan finished enthusiastically.

"Is there a landmark you might recognize so that when you see it, we'll start walking across the fields at the right place?" John asked hopefully.

"No," Susan replied, "but I am pretty confident that I will be able to tell with the satellite map."

John tried to hide his skepticism and to keep a positive mental outlook. *Like these fields don't all look alike,* he thought irritably.

Realizing that there was no choice other than to follow Susan's lead, the Ford Escort continued on the trail for several miles, eventually turning at one point, changing direction.

"This is it," Susan said shortly after the change of direction, "this is where we park and head out through the fields back over to County O. Honestly,

I really don't think that it's too far."

Groaning quietly, Liffey, who always had great difficulty masking her true emotions, tried not to show how reluctant she was to follow Susan's lead.

"I knew this trail would work! Let's ditch the car and find the barn. Then we can walk up a little hill on the side of the barn and set out for the ridge."

Susan had already exited the car when Liffey jumped out after her and said, "Susan, this is not a game. Those dark cars were probably my dad and his secret agent play dates but—maybe not. Maybe they were the bad guys."

"Liffey's right, Susan," John added, stepping out of the car, "we need to take things slowly and not put ourselves out in the open until we figure out what is out there."

A buzzing noise from above quickly caught their attention. What looked like a toy airplane was directly overhead. It hovered for a brief moment before it reversed direction, heading back towards County O.

"Holy Moley!" John exclaimed.

"What *was* that?" Susan asked fearfully.

Liffey and John answered in unison: "A drone!"

At first, Mineral Point's Chief of Police could not help but think that he had received a prank call. After investigating, however, he discovered that, as bizarre and crazy as it seemed, the call had apparently been on the level.

He was still up to his eyeballs dealing with the

aftermath of yesterday's snowstorm and sorting out the Rivers' complaints against Tom Scott who had been taken to the hospital after a maid discovered him in a semi-conscious state at the Mineral Motel. His white truck had disappeared from where it had been abandoned in front of the Scott house and was being treated as a stolen vehicle.

Now he was told he needed to help facilitate the neighboring County Sheriff's department deputies to be on standby, ready to detain a large caravan of people who were going to arrive soon at the New Baltimore Barn.

The agent the Chief had spoken with, suggested that the intruders might be charged with trespassing on private property so they could be detained legally. The Chief was to be definite with the Sheriff's deputies that they were to "step down" and remain only on standby until specifically directed to move in.

The Chief's officer on afternoon patrol duty had called in and reported that there was very little action in town today, just a pink Cadillac coming into the Point on a back road, probably from Dodgeville, which was being followed by a parade of mostly out-of-state vehicles.

"One really strange thing though," the reporting officer said, "Chief, there were three, count em, three Mercedes Benz Ener G Force cars. Remember when we looked at that catalogue and read all about them? And how bummed out we were because we would never be able to afford one for the department?"

"Well, there were three Benz Ener G Force cars in the parade behind that pink Cadillac. Count em. Three."

The federal agent had told the Chief that he worked with Interpol, an agency that never, even in his wildest imagination, the Chief would have ever expected to be working with. The CIA and FBI were also involved.

What in the world was going on here in Mineral Point?

"Well, it looks like we've been discovered," Liffey said calmly. "At least your hair looks amazing, Susan, mine's a disaster."

John tried to act nonchalant, like drones were always following him around, but he felt like any second, his eyes were going to roll back in his head from fear.

Was Liffey serious about her hair?

Since St. Louis, Liffey had become accustomed to running head-on into disastrous, tricky situations and so far, had remained fairly cool-headed in the midst of this one.

"Look guys, so a drone found us and took some pictures and marked our location, so what?"

"Yes," Susan whispered hysterically. "So what?"

"My biggest concern is, WHO is operating it?"

John filled in the blanks. "The good guys or the bad guys?"

"Exactly," Liffey said. "My dad might have been

in one of those big, scary cars and he would be totally snooping around with a drone now if one of those federal agents showed him how to work it."

"I guess I had better call him. I hadn't planned to for awhile but I'm a little worried about that drone. We might be in over our heads if we go sneaking over the fields to the ridge without first comparing notes with my father."

"Do not answer your mobile, Robert. Let it go to messages," Paddlestone ordered when Robert Rivers' phone began chiming like Big Ben.

"You are very groggy and in no shape to have a conversation at the moment. Soon though, you will have to call your daughter and tell her to meet you here with her friends."

"We both know that I particularly need the Scott girl. I think another minute or two to clear your head should suffice."

Robert Rivers was disoriented when he woke up but he was certain that he had never seen this man before who was standing over him.

He would have remembered the flaccid face with the fuzzy unibrow that looked like two connecting black caterpillars. And the hooded, piggy eyes.

He appeared to be approximately five feet tall. *How had such a short person managed to subdue three agents and himself? He must have accomplices…*

"Who are you and how would you know anything about my daughter and her friends?" Robert Rivers demanded.

"Fair questions, Robert," Reginald Paddlestone replied.

"The facts are simple. This adventure began when my staff computer experts detected a simple e-mail concerning the words, 'Gray Dog,' 'Red Rooster' and 'Fox,' along with several other significant words. More about that later though, because time is of the essence here."

"I donned this camouflage costume and joined the party over at your not-so-very safe house where I listened and watched."

"When your wife realized that Liffey had bolted with her two friends and your own sister, you and Maeve discussed what your daughter might be up to."

"I walked slowly right by you and Mrs. Rivers, through that bathroom with the secret door, into the tunnel, where, I will own up, I lurked for awhile, listening to you and Mrs. Rivers having your frantic little conference."

"I will tell you that I still don't have it all down yet, but I learned enough at your house to realize I needed to follow you when you left—and I was ever so right."

"So here we all are," Paddlestone said, grinning like a toothy chimpanzee.

"It is not necessary for you to know my name, Robert."

"Your three friends are asleep on the haystacks in back of you. Parking your cars on the side of this barn was a less than brilliant idea, Robert. I had only to park a bit ahead off the road and, pardon the expression, wait until the right moment arrived to 'take you all out' with my blowpipe. You would still be sleeping like your companions if I had not given you the antidote to my little arrows."

Robert Rivers tried not to over-think his predicament when he realized he was alone with this alarming man. Who knew *what* he had put into the sedative that he had shot everyone up with? For all he knew, this maniac might have used some sort of lethal poison. All of them needed to get medical attention before they found out the hard way that they may have been fatally injured.

"In case you are wondering, I am not planning to harm you, Robert, or anyone else today. I am a chemist and my sleeping remedies are herbal and safe. Although you may feel a bit sore where the projectile pierced your skin."

"I used a clay blowgun still used by natives of the Amazonian rainforests."

"It may be a primitive weapon, but I certainly proved today that it is very effective."

"I do breathing exercises every day to strengthen my respiratory muscles, but today, when you all came so close to me, it was easy-peasy—only four little puffs and America's finest were fast asleep."

"When agent number one opened the side door and walked outside, I stepped behind the open door and waited. The rest of you were easy pickings too. I must say I am not impressed so far with your federal agents. They seem to perform much more effectively in movies."

"Your associates will remain sleeping for another hour or two and my army will be joining me any minute now. However, we still have the problem of not knowing where to look, don't we, Robert? Even though this barn is obviously near our sought-after location."

"Time to call your daughter, Robert. Tell her to meet you immediately here inside the barn with her friends and please don't mention the company you are presently keeping."

Liffey had just worked up the courage to call her father when her phone went off.

She knew she was about to get a long lecture about leaving the house without permission and causing her parents stress.

She deserved harsh words from her father and did regret slipping away and upsetting her parents. She seemed to always be doing this, usually with the best intentions.

"Daddy," Liffey began…. Robert Rivers cut his daughter off abruptly.

"Liffey, I am not upset. I need you to meet me at that barn you told me about. I'm hiding in there now and it's so hot in here it feels like global warming, so please let your mother know you are okay and hurry. We need to get to the ridge before the others, so you must get here as fast as you can."

Paddlestone smiled to himself and smirked.

Robert Rivers had slipped up, just as he hoped he might do, being still under the influence of the powerful rainforest sedative.

Now Paddlestone knew that he was looking for a ridge somewhere near this old barn which greatly simplified the search. He had done his homework en route from Beijing. He was now in what was called the 'Driftless Area,' where there were ridges almost everywhere one looked.

Hopefully there not multiple ridges near this particular barn, Paddlestone thought. *There is no time for that.*

Any minute now, when his team arrived, they could begin searching the surrounding fields for the right ridge.

After locating limestone rock formations, things would move along quickly because he had brought several magnetic anomaly detectors with him to search for the hidden, mostly metallic equipment.

This entire operation should take no time at all. Then he would be off to Milwaukee and his private jet.

He thought he might have some German cuisine catered to the airport hangar for the long flight home. He had heard that one could have excellent sauerbraten in Milwaukee. Cabbage rolls or some bratwurst and sauerkraut might also be nice. Or maybe rabbit—he could not think of the German word for 'rabbit.'

Perhaps he could actually bring some bratwurst home with him to China from one of the restaurants. He had eaten one once in Germany and thought they tasted reasonably good.

Robert Rivers could hardly believe it when the deranged little man called information in Milwaukee inquiring about carry-out food from Mader's German Restaurant. What kind of nut case was he?

Liffey ended the call with her father and bit her lip.

If he's not totally furious with me now, then something is really, really wrong. He told me to call mother and to hurry. And—he had said 'global warming.'

'They' had her dad at the New Baltimore Barn.

228

CHAPTER THIRTY-TWO
A Parade

Dustin Fields looked in the rearview mirror. All that was needed now was a marching band and a few floats and he would have a real parade. It was hard not to feel a bit unsettled. Who *were* all those people following him?

Finally, he could no longer put up with having no idea whatsoever about why he was driving around in a pink Cadillac with three ladies headed nowhere in particular—except perhaps eventually to Jean Rivers' new house to discuss 'fang shwee,' whatever that was. Liffey had told him that her mother would tell him what to do and when he needed to do it.

Jean Rivers had to have figured out by now that they were not going to her beauty shop appointment. She probably thought she had been kidnapped.

It came as a big surprise when the entire parade

began reversing direction after performing orderly U-turns from rear to front, one by one, leaving the pink Cadillac all by itself. After Dustin had adjusted to having gone from leader of the pack to parade 'caboose,' he welcomed the change.

Ever since he had seen a 1970's movie about a mile-long truck convoy, he had always imagined what it would be like to be part of one. Saying things like: "10-4 Good Buddy" on his CB radio when one of the other truckers notified him that he had spotted a 'bear,' which was a police car waiting to bust speeding trucks.

This, however, was not anything at all how he had imagined his convoy would be—driving a pink Cadillac with three old ladies, but it was probably the closet he would ever get to actually being in a real one.

He did a U-Turn, accelerated, and followed the new parade.

The ladies did not protest.

After Liffey had delivered the grim news about her father to John and Susan, she called Harry at the safe house and asked him to mobilize the other federal agents who had stayed behind to interrogate Louise.

"So then, I say we start to make our way across these fields and, like we all decided, just wing it," John said when Liffey turned back to him.

"I agree," Liffey said. "We don't have a lot of options here and we can't wait until the other agents turn up—it has got to be at least an eight minute drive to get out here from town."

Susan looked ill, like she was going to start hyperventilating again, but declared passionately that she was "in."

Liffey tried not to think about what she might find in the barn. Not knowing how many people were in there with her father was the worst part. What if there were lots?

Yet so far, throughout this entire drama, she still had not seen one, single 'bad guy.' Was everybody just imagining that someone else was actively looking for the gold mine and whatever else might be there?

Except for Louise, which still seemed hard to believe, there had been no ugly confrontations. But Louise was working for *someone*. And Robert Rivers was now being held prisoner by *someone*.

The fields were not as muddy as they had feared and they were able to make good time, traveling swiftly in spite of the soggy earth. Within five minutes, the New Baltimore Barn came into view, sitting on top of a not-so-faraway mound.

"Let's sprint guys. I am so worried about my dad," Liffey shouted, racing ahead. She had just gone out of sight when John and Susan, trying to keep up, heard a high-pitched scream of: "Noooo!"

John raced ahead and discovered Liffey looking shell-shocked, standing at the bottom of a small slope by the bank of a narrow, fast flowing river.

"How are we supposed to get across this thing?"

she asked in a high-pitched, frustrated voice.

Another voice coming from some twenty feet to their left, spoke up: "Well, I say we cross this water, which by the way is the Pecatonica River, on this fat downed tree branch," Susan suggested.

Liffey and John managed to laugh and lined up behind Susan who deftly led them across.

When they were directly across County O from the impressive two-storey building that said, **NEW BALTIMORE 1838**, Liffey paused to study the barn. There were four windows on the first level that was completely stone, facing the road.

The two dark cars they had avoided earlier were parked alongside the barn on the left.

The second level looked like traditional barn wood, painted red. There were no windows but she knew there would be at least one door on each side of the upper barn and a small one, up high in the very back of the barn, for tossing loose hay up into the loft. *All old barns have a door leading into a hayloft,* Liffey thought.

"We can't risk the possibility that somebody could be looking through one of those four windows and see us strolling across the street. So, we'll go through the muck on the other side of the road, and come at the barn from the side," Liffey decided.

"Let's go! My dad sounded funny," Liffey said apprehensively, taking off running again.

"I'm sure *my* dad will get the Feds here within another minute or so," Susan called after her.

232

"Maybe you should keep out of sight and wait for them, Susan. Otherwise, they might be walking into an ambush," John said, as he ran after Liffey.

Susan nodded and watched as Liffey and John jogged across County Trunk O to the muddy field on the other side of the road.

"Enough," the Chief muttered to himself after his deputy reported the change in both the parade's direction and lineup. He had promised the Interpol agent he would not call in Lafayette County law enforcement until he got the go ahead but his deputy said that she had a "vibe" something was going down right now and he trusted her sixth sense. She said that there was a helicopter heading in the direction of County Trunk O where the parade had turned just past the Kwick Trip.

"And I'm supposed to tell the Sheriff exactly *what*?" the Chief started up, talking to the walls in the empty police station. "That a pink Cadillac, which had at first been followed by a line of cars, is now no longer the leader of the pack?"

"Now, the Caddie is a follower? I'll be a laughing stock. Go to the New Baltimore Barn immediately and arrest the drivers in a parade of probably legally driven vehicles? It's not exactly a parade without a permit."

But I am not messing around with the Feds, the Chief thought. *I am glad whatever is going down now is at least happening in another county.*

The Mineral Point officer who had notified the Chief, joined the parade, directly behind the pink Cadillac.

The Chief's phone lit up. He dreaded answering yet another call. If this one was also about the pink car, he was going to retire early.

He listened briefly and then told the dispatcher he was heading over to County Trunk O. He also told her to call the Lafayette Sheriff's Department to get their deputies over to the New Baltimore Barn.

The Mineral Point High School Principal had just reported that Susan Scott and Liffey Rivers had not shown up for classes today and could not be located. It seemed that neither the girls nor their parents were answering their phones.

The recently plowed-up farm field next to the New Baltimore Barn was almost impossible to wade through. Deep, thick mud was sucking at their feet like quicksand, drastically slowing Liffey and John's progress.

Liffey was almost despairing, thinking that they probably should have risked crossing over the road directly in front of the barn windows to have avoided this problem, when she heard a dog barking.

"John, what are we going to do? We can barely get one foot in front of the other and now there's a dog barking from somewhere straight ahead of us. Someone from inside the barn is bound to hear it and come out and see us."

"I don't hear a dog, Liffey," John replied.

"How can you not hear it? It's..."

Liffey could not believe what she was now both hearing and *seeing*.

It was the gray dog from above the sidewalk, but it was alive now, not a shadow like the one that had been on the snow. It had almost reached them when John turned around and said, "Exactly where is this barking coming from, Liffey?"

Liffey did not seem to be aware of John's talking to her as she extended her hand to greet the gray dog. He licked it like they knew each other well.

I have jumped off the cliff again, she thought. *Aunt Jean said it can happen more than once if things get to be too stressful for you. You just start hallucinating, acting crazy, and then you are sent away to rest. Here goes!*

Liffey could feel her feet beginning to move forward effortlessly now, following the dog.

She moved past John, who was still stuck in the mud, and began running towards the barn while he stood watching, stupefied.

The gray dog led her to the back of the barn, where he raised a paw and leaned forward, his nose pointing directly at a tall man who was waiting for her, leaning against the building next to a small ladder which led up to an old weathered door. Liffey knew it would open into an old hayloft.

She smiled at the man, fully aware that later she would be freaking out about what had happened here today.

The man was pale and scruffy-looking. He had a prominent nose, patches of facial hair and a strong chin. He was wearing drab, dirty gray clothes and a shapeless hat but no shoes. His large, blue eyes were luminous, like they might glow in the dark. There was purple bruising on his neck.

He looked tired, but friendly, and extended the same arm Liffey recognized as being the one which had held the Red Rooster's door open for her in the blizzard yesterday.

Her new friend helped steady the ladder as Liffey pulled her muddy shoes off and got her footing. He held it for her as she climbed up and opened the tiny, weathered door leading into the hayloft.

She walked soundlessly across the hayloft's old floor boards. Because of her Irish dance training, she could not only walk, but jump up and land without making a sound.

Below, she could hear a man's voice shouting at her father, in a cultured British accent, telling him that his volunteer army was only minutes away now and he demanded to know the location of the gold mine before 'they' arrived.

Liffey was sick and tired of not knowing who 'they' were. There had to be at least three "theys" by now.

Her father kept repeating that he did not know where Liffey or Susan were and that he was not going to call Liffey again.

Liffey tried not to think about the nice, helpful barefoot man outside with his gray dog. She might have to talk to a psychiatrist someday about who that man might have been and what she thought she had seen.

Right now, she needed to save her father.

There were bales of hay stacked up in front and in back of the partially bald, short man. His back was to the hayloft.

Her father was sitting on one of the haystacks, directly in front of the man. In back of her father, there were three federal agents who seemed to be totally passed out, sleeping on other haystacks. What had this lone man done to them?

Like an answer to an unsaid prayer, she saw a long rope dangling down from the ceiling, only a foot or so in front of her. Children had probably used it many years ago to swing themselves over to the other side of the barn where they would drop down onto a pile of soft hay.

"I think you are lying, Robert. I think you told your daughter in code not to come. I normally do not employ drastic measures, but I am warning you that you are only seconds away from some very dire consequences."

Liffey had heard enough. She backed up, got a running start, grabbed the rope and launched herself from the hayloft.

As she sailed across the room towards the creepy man who was threatening her father, she slid down the rope, lowering herself a few feet to better position herself, making sure she would land on her target from behind.

She dropped on him like a bomb released from an airplane. He fell to the floor, crying out in pain.

Seconds later, while Liffey was trying to process what she had just done and what she should do next, another body came flying through the air from the hayloft.

It was John, who had managed to unglue himself from the mud field and make it to the barn.

He landed on the floor next to the man and began to tie Reginald Paddlestone's hands behind his back.

"Well you certainly came prepared, young man," Robert Rivers said with a grateful smile.

"Yes you certainly did! Where did you get the rope?" Liffey asked.

John pulled a Swiss Army knife from his pocket. "I cut off a piece of the Tarzan vine upstairs." *Of course*, Liffey remembered. *His trusty knife!*

He pulled Reginald Paddlestone up and on to his knees but before anyone had time to ask questions, a side door burst open and the camouflaged National Guardsmen from the safe house moved in, this time like experienced commandos. Liffey was impressed.

They were followed by Harry Scott, still wearing his bathrobe, Susan, and the other federal agents.

Louise had already been taken to Madison for further questioning.

Helicopters hovered above the barn. Everyone seemed to have arrived at the same time.

Outside, a megaphone was ordering the parade of cars to stop and barriers were erected. Two parade vehicles tried to make a run for it but Lafayette County Sheriff's deputies chased them, forcing them to pull over.

Protocol dictated that other counties respond to major unfolding events and sirens could be heard coming down O from both directions.

John sat down on a haystack and watched the grand finale.

It was hard to believe that he had only been in Wisconsin since early this morning.

Paramedics came in with stretchers and started transporting the sleeping Feds to waiting ambulances, assisted by National Guardsmen.

"Welcome to the Liffey Rivers reality show, John," Liffey said. "I've got to say that you seem to fit right in!" Liffey beamed a smile from the nearby haystack where she was sitting with her exhausted father, holding his hand.

Susan was standing next to Harry.

She was white as a sheet, but obviously high on adrenaline. Liffey could hear her chattering on like fast fingers on a keyboard.

Ann, Maeve, Aunt Jean and Dustin were finally brought into the barn for questioning.

"It's going to be dark before long," Liffey worried. "Can we at least go outside and try to find the ridge before sunset, Daddy?"

"I don't see how that would be possible, Liffey," Robert Rivers answered, waving to his wife who had managed to break away from her CIA interrogator and was crossing over to him.

"We will each need to give a statement to more people than you can imagine, Liffey."

"The CIA and FBI, Interpol—all of them will want to find the gold mine along with whatever Mr. Brit thinks is hidden inside it. Then each agency will give itself credit for their discovery. If you somehow manage to get by all those agents, stay in range for questioning."

She nodded at John who poked Susan in the shoulder and gestured at her to come with Liffey and himself.

Susan managed to slip away when her mother joined her father on his haystack.

The three of them made their way nonchalantly over to the inactive side of the barn and sauntered out through one of the side doors.

It was obvious that there was very little daylight left. Liffey figured they had to find the right ridge within twenty minutes, max.

It was going to be very difficult, not only finding the right ridge, but figuring out which part of it to concentrate their depleted energy levels on.

So far, it had been a very long day.

CHAPTER THIRTY-THREE
The Barefoot Man

L iffey looked around for the barefoot man. She wanted to thank him for his help, even though she knew he might only be a figment of her imagination, but he had vanished. She decided to decide later whether or not she would share that encounter with John and Susan.

She might talk to Maeve though. She had to remember that now she had a sympathetic mother for the awkward kind of conversations that would more than likely make her father think she needed a shrink.

He had already made her go to a therapist for years because he thought she had coulrophobia, a morbid fear of clowns. This was probably true, but what was a therapist supposed to do about it?

She just made sure to avoid clowns whenever possible and close her eyes if she did unexpectedly run into one. She had only physically attacked two clowns before in her life-to-date and both of those clowns had totally deserved it. One of them had terrorized her during a clown parade when she was five by squirting her pink patent leather shoes with water while he grinned at her and activated a loud siren. The other clown had, as she had suspected, turned out to be a criminal.

It was frightening to even imagine what her father might do now if she told him she thought she might be seeing a dead man and that the dead man had a gray dog that was the same dog from Mineral Point standing on the pedestal downtown—Mineral Point's mascot.

The November sky looked like it was not going to host daylight for much longer when they arrived at the limestone ridge, about two city blocks from the New Baltimore Barn.

"There it is!" Susan was ecstatic as she pointed to an exposed area of limestone about three feet high and, like she had described before, about as long as a football field.

"I cannot believe I thought I had been so high up off the ground when Uncle William brought me here," she laughed, starting to move off towards it.

"Okay, Susan. Calm down," Liffey said, reaching for her friend's arm to restrain her.

"First, you must try to imagine where 'Stir-Tea' is. Close your eyes and try to relax. Imagine that your uncle is right here with you..."

Liffey abruptly stopped talking.

The barefoot man was here again with his dog. They were directly above the ridge at what Liffey thought would be around the fifty yard line in a football field. They were floating about six inches above the limestone.

The man beckoned her to come over to him and Liffey found herself obeying, without questioning why or what she was doing.

John and Susan were light years away. She had forgotten all about them.

When she made it to the fifty yard line, the man smiled and mouthed a silent "thank you" before he and his dog disappeared again.

"It's right here," Liffey whispered. Then she shouted: "It's right here where I'm standing!"

Susan was incredulous. "Are you sure, Liffey? I think it's a bit farther down the ridge. In fact, I'm positive."

Liffey did not acknowledge Susan, who had already walked past her and was now almost at the other end of the ridge. Instead, she started studying the rock formation in front of her in the fading light.

She bent over and put both of her hands on the damp rock. She closed her eyes and rubbed the cold stone with the palms of her hand like she was giving the ridge a massage.

John, wondering if he should be disturbed by this display of affection for a rock formation, made an inquiry: "Liffey, why are you touching the rock like it's a kitten or puppy or…"

"This is why, John," Liffey interrupted, pulling him over next to her and placing his hands on top of the limestone.

"Close your eyes, and let me move your hands for you," she instructed.

"It's the rebus picture puzzle!" John yelled loudly, trying unsuccessfully to restrain himself. "This is totally awesome, Liffey!"

"Susan, come here! Hurry!" Liffey beckoned.

Susan, looking annoyed and very put out to have been disturbed while she was searching, walked back to her friends reluctantly.

"Look, guys, I really need to concentrate if we are ever going to find the right spot," she said impatiently.

"Give me your hands, Susan, Liffey said.

"Liffey, really, I don't have time to play games with you now. It's almost dark. We are finally so close and…" Liffey cut her off. "Exactly, Susan. We are so close that…"

Susan stomped away indignantly.

John shrugged and Liffey asked him to go and get her own and Susan's parents.

Then she ran her hands again over the words, **STIR-TEA SUSAN** which were carved deeply into the stone, below the outline of a tea cup and saucer with a spoon.

"Phew," Liffey gulped, somewhat overwhelmed.

"Susan," Liffey called again, "you *really* need to get over here right now!"

"I will when I'm good and ready, Liffey. Now please stop bossing me around and leave me alone!"

It flashed across Liffey's petty side, the side she always tried not to give into, not to tell Susan why she had to "get right over here." But that would be mean. *Really bad karma for me,* Liffey thought.

"Susan, get over here! It's here. **STIR-TEA** is right here where I'm standing."

A CIA forensic discovery team had been called in from Milwaukee to begin the search for the 're-located' counterfeiting paraphernalia, using powerful outdoor flood lights to illuminate the Sir-Tea location that Liffey had let Susan 'discover.' Interpol agents from Chicago had also arrived and were questioning Mr. Paddlestone, who was much more distressed now about his not being able to claim "private property" than the reality of how much trouble he was in.

The FBI agents busied themselves interrogating the people from the parade of cars who were being held inside the barn, carefully guarded by Sheriff's deputies. As had been requested by Interpol agents, Federal U.S. Marshals were en route with a bus to transfer the parade people to Chicago for processing.

Everybody was very busy at the moment except Liffey Rivers. It was understood that she was always to remain 'anonymous,' even though the Skunk Man was probably gone forever. But if that were the case, then why had her father built such an elaborate safe house underneath their home in Mineral Point? It seemed to Liffey like it was an extreme precaution to take—unless there was a real concern that she and her mother might still be on their enemy's radar?

She was very relieved that this present ordeal was finally over with but kept thinking about the man and his gray dog. Susan had casually mentioned at the Red Rooster yesterday that the Scott family was related to William Caffee, the man who had been hanged in 1842 in Mineral Point. Liffey had seen the purple bruising on the neck of the man who had helped her today.

Susan had told her that for years the town had declared November first, "Hanging Day," like it was some kind of public holiday that should be celebrated.

So maybe William Caffee takes a stroll each year on his anniversary. Maybe this year he wanted to help his mother's Scott relatives? Liffey thought.

Yesterday had been the anniversary of his public execution on that first of November, so long ago. *Was he going through me to help Susan?* Liffey wondered.

Robert Rivers had arranged for the Scott family's attorney to come to the site to make sure that their ownership of the long vein of gold running through a vast deposit of quartz embedded in the limestone ridge, was sorted out properly.

After the evidence team had carefully cut and removed the large slab of stone with the **STIR-TEA SUSAN** art work, they had also discovered a wide, deep hole, lined with thick plastic, which contained

Reginald Paddlestone's counterfeiting paraphernalia.

On top of the thick plastic, there was a manila envelope addressed to the 'Harry Scott Family' from 'William Arthur Scott, Address Unknown.'

The lead investigator adjusted his gloves and carefully opened the envelope. Before he formally entered the contents into evidence, he called the Scotts over and began to read:

Dear Harry, Ann And Susan,

I am indeed very much dead if you are reading this letter now. Dead as dead can be, as it were.

Congratulations, Susan! I knew you would figure out STIR-TEA and guide your parents to this place.

The gold vein here should keep you all busy for a long time to come. I discovered the gold deposit the day after Susan's Y dousing stick went haywire.

There had always been a legend in the Scott family that William Caffee, the son of Elizabeth Scott Caffee, who was executed in 1842, had found gold embedded in quartz just a few weeks before he shot a man over at Gratiot's Grove. But he ran off to Saint Louis and when the bounty hunters found him, he was never again a free man. Apparently, the person or people he had told about the gold, had not believed him.

Now, as to some peculiar equipment buried in this hole. Harry, it needs to get to the FEDS asap. I did not take action to turn it over because it was my life insurance policy. I will try to explain.

I went, as you all must now know, undercover in China for some years. There is a club known as The Fox and Hounds in Beijing. There had been rumors that this club was involved with some shady enterprises but I discovered its only real purpose was a plot to flood Europe with counterfeit British pounds. The equipment I have hidden here after drilling down through solid limestone, might have successfully accomplished the mission of a Reginald Paddlestone, the man who was only months away from wreaking havoc on much of the world, when I managed to sabotage his life's ambition by stealing his plates and other contraptions. I also have his computer program applications down in the hole, but he assuredly has his own files backed up somewhere.

I knew Paddlestone would be after me like the cartoon Fox riding the horse in my codicil riddle that led you here, but that you, Harry, the Gray Dog (I always knew your code name but never let on) and myself, the Red Rooster, would ultimately defeat him and I knew that so long as the equipment remained hidden, I would remain alive.

I hoped Susan would figure out this location and I knew that Harry would suspect that there might be more to my codicil than a map to a gold mine and that it was a matter of international importance. I left Chinese symbols and drew the £ sign and bankers cartoon to help you make the connection. It is remarkable that Susan solved the anagram.

There are bankers in London and other places who collaborated with Paddlestone, standing ready to circulate the phony money when he provided them with it. The names of the suspect bankers are in the smaller envelope in this packet addressed to, THE GRAY DOG.

I guess you could say this is our final spy moment, Harry. Please turn over the list in the envelope to my former boss. I so very much wished that we would have been able to talk shop throughout our lives of espionage. But working for separate agencies would not allow it.

One more thing. I want to clear up some family history before I sign off forever.

I am the great-great nephew of Paul Scott who lived in this area from the 1830's until his death in 1866, shortly after the Civil War ended.

His wife, Catherine McDermott Scott, followed him to the grave six years after his death. He had two children-Patrick Michael Scott and Jane Elizabeth Scott. The Scotts inherited their land and property in Wisconsin from Catherine's sister, Mary McDermott, who had fled Ireland when she married a wealthy protestant, the son of their landlord in Sligo. Neither her husband's nor her own family could accept what they had done—marrying 'out of their own faith.' Those were dark times. Paul had met Catherine in Sligo when he had gone back to visit his dying mother who had refused to emigrate to America. They fell in love and were married. Mary and her husband both died of cholera and their extensive land in Wisconsin was bequeathed to Catherine, Mary's sister. Catherine and Paul left Ireland after their children were born in Sligo and took up farming here.

Jane Scott entered the Sinsinawa Dominican Sisters in 1850, shortly after their order was founded in 1847 by Father Samuel Mazzuchelli. She taught school for many years and retired to the Motherhouse on the Sinsenawa Mound until her death in 1897. Sister Roberta Ann—I never could understand why nuns used to take a new name when they entered the convent, left all of this ancestor information I have disclosed here in this letter. It is in the box of cartoons I gave Susan long ago.

Patrick Scott was injured fighting at the Second Battle of Bull Run. He was with the 7th Wisconsin Volunteer Infantry Regiment. He returned to the family farm and married a local girl—Mary Southwick. They farmed the Scott land until they got lost in the mists of time. I never found out what happened to them except that they had three sons. I am the great nephew of the son they called 'Paul' who was named after Patrick's father.

One more thing. I think that William Caffee fellow might still be around the Point. He was a Scott. His mother Elizabeth Scott died when he was around eight. I think I saw him once, a few years ago, crossing barefoot over Commerce Street with a gray dog. He sat down near the stream that runs next to the place where he had been hanged. I am fairly certain that this happened on a November 1st, the anniversary of his hanging.

I am most thankful for all of you and the love and care you unfailingly always gave to me, your eccentric Uncle William. Susan, just in case you were wondering, they do serve Figgy Hobbin up here in Heaven. I will save a piece for you.   Until we all meet again,

William Arthur Scott AKA The Red Rooster

CHAPTER THIRTY-FOUR
The Mineral Point Feis

Aunt Jean had finally convinced Liffey that there were no rules at Irish dancing competitions which specifically excluded wearing wings. She pointed out that there were capes on back of most school and solo dresses, so why not inflatable wings?

"I am an adult Irish dancer, Liffey darling. My creativity must be allowed to be fully expressed. You'll see. I will create a trend. Enough of those crystals and shiny beads. Irish dancing will look to Mother Nature for inspiration from now on—thanks entirely to me and my artistic leadership."

On the upside, at least Aunt Jean won't look like a sputtering sparkler whirling around on stage in her new solo dress, Liffey thought. *It could be way worse.*

Aunt Jean's new dress was entirely black silk and its hidden wings were exact copies of Monarch Butterfly wings with their orange, white and black pattern.

"I will begin my steps trapped in my cocoon," Jean began, "after I emerge and begin to fly, I will do a few butterflies and then release the wings."

Liffey decided it would be best to somehow prevent her mother from coming to the Fall Feis, as Maeve had little patience for Aunt Jean's theatrical stunts. John was going to have to miss the feis too because he had to return to New Hampshire.

He had invited Liffey and her family to try skiing

in New Hampshire and her parents said that a family trip would be good for Neil. Even Aunt Jean planned to come along.

Aunt Jean had still not told Maeve that she had purchased a downtown building in Mineral Point for her new Irish dance school. Liffey promised her aunt she would tell Maeve when she thought the timing was right. Maybe her mother would enjoy having her own official Irish dance academy? She was a TCRG after all.

Everything would fall into place sooner or later. Maybe Sinead McGowan could even come over next summer from Sligo for the Mineral Point Feis that Aunt Jean was plotting. Her catchy slogan for this competition was going to be: "Get the LEAD out of your feet at the Mineral Point Feis."

After the Fall Feis next weekend, Liffey decided she was going to turn her attention to investigating the vampire stories Susan had told her.

Since there was already a ghost living in Mineral Point since 1842, then why not a vampire?

THE END

GLOSSARY

AESOP'S FABLES: The Greek storyteller, Aesop, was born in approximately 620 B.C. Tradition says he was born a slave and he developed a real talent for telling fables that were widely used to teach truths with morals in a simple, understandable way.

AVE: The Hail Mary, or **Ave Maria** (Pronounced Ah-Vay. Latin for Hail Mary) is a prayer to Mary, the Mother of Jesus and along with the Our Father, Glory Be, and other prayers, is the main part of the Catholic Rosary devotion.

BADGERS: The name 'Badger' State for Wisconsin had its origin in the lead mining districts of Southwestern Wisconsin. Miners who came from great distances who could not travel home for the winters, burrowed into the sides of the bluffs and hills like badgers. These 'dugout' dwellings made them permanent residents of the Wisconsin Territory.

BUTTERFLIES IN IRISH DANCING:

A butterfly is a difficult Irish dance step in which the dancer jumps high, keeping both feet underneath, and switches the feet positions mid-air, keeping them close together. Flickers or quivers are sometimes done while switching feet. Or, the feet can be flattened doing the switches. Liffey practices these advanced steps holding on to two weighted-down chairs. Hard shoe butterflies use the "flat feet" version, and the dancer usually does a heel click while switching feet. Tricky footwork.

CORNWALL: Cornwall is the farthest southwest county in England located on the large southwestern peninsula that divides the English Channel on the south from the Irish Sea on the north.

COUSIN JACKS: The nickname for the miners from Cornwall who lived in Mineral Point in the 1800's.

COUSIN JENNYS: The nickname for the Cornish women who lived in Mineral Point in the 1800's.

DOWSING STICK: Some lead miners used a Y-shaped, forked sapling stick, taken from a willow or hazelnut tree, to look, or go 'prospecting' for lead deposits. This ancient method has many critics but also many believers.

FENG SHUI: Ancient Chinese philosophical practice of treating space like a living organism. To keep living space healthy, energy must be able to circulate throughout the environment. This energy is called 'chi.'

Feis(fesh): A traditional Gaelic arts and culture festival usually meaning an Irish dance competition. Plural: Feiseanna.

This engraving of the statue we know as Morley's Dog comes from the original J.W. Fiske catalog of products.

GRAY DOG: The Gray Pointer Dog of Mineral Point was probably purchased by mail from a catalogue entitled: *Zinc Animals: Deer, Dogs, Lions, Etc. J.W. Fiske Iron Works NYC, 1874.* There is an identical drawing of this dog in this sales brochure listed as "No. 271 French Blood Hound Zinc." However, French Bloodhounds have long ears that almost touch their nose. The dog in Mineral Point, is definitely a Pointer. An identical dog, Morley, was swept away in the Johnstown Flood in 1889.

HORNPIPE: In the Irish dancing tradition, a Hornpipe has 4/4 time and is danced wearing hard shoes. Some say it is the ancestor of modern tap dancing.

INTERPOL: The world's largest international police organization with 200 member countries enabling police all around the world to work together to solve crimes.

1840 MINERAL POINT MAP: LEAD MINES

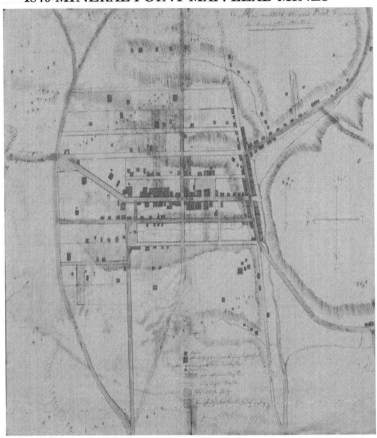

The tiny dots represent mines in Mineral Point in 1840. The larger dots are buildings. High Street is the most densely housed street running left to right at the center. Today in Mineral Point and its environs, there are still abandoned, lost mines. In 1830, Mineral Point was the largest city in what later became the Wisconsin Territory.

PASSENGER PIGEONS: North American pigeons that lived in enormous migratory flocks until the early 20th century, when hunting and destruction of their habitat led to their becoming extinct. One of the largest ever recorded migratory flock measured 1 mile wide and 300 miles long and took 14 hours to pass.

PENDARVIS: In 1970 the Wisconsin Historical Society acquired the group of stone Cornish miners' houses in Mineral Point known as Pendarvis, named after an estate in Cornwall. The houses were originally restored in the 1930's by Robert Neal and Edgar Hellum. After acquiring the properties, the Historical Society began establishing a historic site interpreting the history of Cornish settlement and the days when Mineral Point was a rough lead mining area. Costumed interpreters offer guided tours through the Pendarvis complex. Pendarvis is open year-round for pre-arranged group tours, events and field trips, and daily to the public from May through October.
http://mineralpoint.com/history/pendarvis-historic-site

REBUS PUZZLE: A puzzle or riddle made up of pictures, letters or symbols whose names sound like the parts or syllables of a word or phrase.

SAINT PATRICK: The Patron Saint of Ireland.

SAINT PIRAN: Patron Saint of Cornwall who came to England from Ireland. Cornwall's black & white flag design is said to have originated from Saint Piran's hearthstone when tin in the stone melted and left the cross pattern.

SCAT: Solid matter (AKA: Poop) discharged from an animal's alimentary canal that has become petrified. Some people collect it.

SHA CHI: A house is in a state of sha chi if energy within the environment is overactive or depleted.

SHENG CHI: In practicing Feng Shui, Sheng Chi is achieved when energy is in balance within a house.

Slán: Farewell in Irish. Pronounced 'Slawn.'

SLIP JIG: The Slip Jig is a soft shoe Irish dance step in 9/8 time. Along with the reel, jig and hornpipe, it is one the four most common steps performed at an Irish dance competition, or 'feis.' (pronounced fesh)

SUCKERS: Miners in Mineral Point who came from the south—mostly Illinois, who worked in the lead mines during the summer and headed south for the winter, migrating like suckers, a species of fish, which traveled south before the winter freeze set in. Unlike 'Badgers,' accepted as a nickname by Wisconsin people, Illinois (understandably) rejected the nickname 'Suckers.'

TCRG: A Commission Certified Irish Dance Teacher. In Irish: Teagascóir Choimisiúin le Rinci Gaelacha.

UK: The United Kingdom is made up of England, Scotland, Wales and six counties of Northern Ireland.

WISCONSIN TERRITORY: Before it became a state in 1848, the Wisconsin Territory was established in 1836. It included all of Wisconsin, Iowa, Minnesota and the part of the Dakotas east of the Missouri River. The governor in 1842, James Duane Doty, wanted it spelled **'Wiskonsin,'** because he thought that spelling better represented the Native American word for the longest river in the area, but it did not catch on.

SOURCES

Aesop, (1867). "The Fox, the Rooster, and the Dog". *Aesop's Fables* (Lit2Go Edition). Retrieved March 11, 2014 http://etc.usf.edu/lit2go/35/aesops-fables/597/the-fox-the-rooster-and-the-dog/

Beall, Herman & Barbara. *Mineral Point Wisconsin.* Arcadia Publishing. Chicago, 2000.

Beaman, Frank. *Guidebook to Historic Preservation In Mineral Point, Wisconsin.* Mineral Point Historic Preservation Commission and Little Creek Press. Mineral Point, WI, 2011.

Breihan, Bill. Captain Fortunatis Berry. "Looking Backwards," (Volume XVII, No. 2, Summer, 1998), Lafayette County Historical Society, Darlington, WI.

Brennan, Helen. *The Story of Irish Dance.* Roberts Rinehart. Lanham, Maryland, 2001.

Davenport, Don. "Rock Cornish Dens: Mineral Point Offers Taste of Early Wisconsin," *Chicago Tribune News,* 1995.

Derleth, August. *The Hills Stand Watch.* Duell, Sloan & Pearce. New York, 1960.

Fiedler, George. *Mineral Point: A History.* Mineral Point

Historical Society and Iowa County Democrat Tribune. (1962).

"The Hanging of William Caffee," Parts 1 through 4, Billingham, Ryan. *The Democrat Tribune*. Mineral Point, Wisconsin, November, 2006.

History of Iowa County. Western Historical Company. Chicago, MDCCCLXXXI.

Holland, Stanley T. with Johnson, James. *A History of Mining In Iowa County*. Iowa County Historical Society.

Holmes, Fred L., Sketches by Max Fernekes, *Old World Wisconsin, Around Europe In The Badger State*. E.M. Hale & Company. Eau Claire, Wisconsin 1944.

Iowa County 1842 Wisconsin Territorial Census Ranges 1 & 2, Western Division.

"Lead Mining in Wisconsin, It's been carried on for three-quarters of a century," *Milwaukee Sentinel*. February 23, 1902, p. 14.

Mazzuchelli, Samuel. *Memoirs: historical and edifying, of a missionary apostolic of the order of Saint Dominic among various Indian tribes and among the Catholics and Protestants in the United States of America*. William F. Hall Printing Company. Chicago, 1915 Edition.

Pendarvis Endowment Trust Fund. 4th Edition. Mineral

Point, Wisconsin, 1999.

Pfotenhauer, Nancy. *A Field Guide to Mineral Point*. Little Creek Press. Mineral Point, Wisconsin, 2000.

Price, Kay & Hendricks, Marian. *Mineral Point*. Arcadia Publishing. Chicago, 2008.

Norman, Beth Scott & Michael. *Haunted Heartland*. Stanton & Lee Publishers, Inc. Madison, Wisconsin, 1985

Smith, Alice Elizabeth. *James Duane Doty, Frontier Promoter*. State Historical Society of Wisconsin, 1954

Thwaites, Reuben Gold. Collections State Historical Society of Wisconsin. Vol. XV Company, State Printer. Madison, WI, 1900.

"William Caffee – Part one of Trial 9/23/1842 in Wisconsin for the murder of Samuel Southwick," *North Western Gazette & Galena Advertiser*. Galena, Illinois, Friday, September 23, 1842.

"William Caffee – Part two of Trial for the murder of Samuel Southwick in WI," *North Western Gazette & Galena Advertiser*. Galena, Illinois, Friday, September 30, 1842.

Wisconsin: comprising sketches of counties, towns, events, institutions, and persons, arranged in encyclopedic form, ed. By Ex-Gov. Geo. W. Peck (Madison, Wis., Western Historical Association, 1906).

Wisconsin Historical Society Online:

1. Weather on November 1, 1842.
   Record From Fort Winnebago Daily Log.

2. 1840 Map of Lead Mines in Mineral Point.

3. 1837 Featherstone's account of Mineral Point.

Wisconsin Temperance Journal Vol. I. Milwaukee. April, 1840.

Wyman, Mark. *Wisconsin Frontier.* Bloomington: Indiana University Press, 1998.

MANY THANKS TO:

Mineral Point Library Archives Curators Mary Alice Moore & Nancy Pfotenhauer & Library Director, Barbara Polizzi. Also to Loren Farrey for helping with the New Baltimore Barn, the McCoy Public Library in Shullsburg, WI, with its extensive Father Samuel Mazuchelli resources and especially to author T. Evan Williams, for his endless research and always helpful input.

OTHER BOOKS BY BRENNA BRIGGS

The Mystery of the Sparkling Solo Dress Crown

The Mystery of the Winking Judge

The Secret of the Mountain of the Moon

In the Shadow of the Serpent

The Alaskan Sun

Four Mini Mysteries

BROCKAGH BOOKS
WWW.LIFFEYRIVERS.COM